CW00530864

SIX
WAGGING
TALES

SIX

WAGGING

TALES

My 50 Years with Guide Dogs

by Joyce Dudley, as told to Brian Frost

with a Preface by

Rt Hon David Blunkett MP

© Copyright 2004
Joyce Dudley

The right of Joyce Dudley to be identified as
author of this work has been asserted by her in accordance with Copyright, Designs
and Patents Act 1988

All rights reserved. No reproduction,
copy or transmission of this publication may be made
without written permission. No paragraph of this publication may be reproduced,
copied or transmitted
save with the written permission or in accordance
with the provisions of the Copyright Act 1956 (as amended). Any person who does any
unauthorised act
in relation to this publication may be liable
to criminal prosecution and civil
claims for damage.

Paperback ISBN 1 903970 56 3

Produced
by

Central Publishing Services
Royd Street Offices
Milnsbridge
Huddersfield
West Yorkshire
HD3 4QY

www.centralpublishing.co.uk

Contents

Preface

Joyce Dudley's book touches a chord, as it will with all readers.

The cheerful and endearing title is a good indication of the joy both engendered for her and for the four-legged friends, which are the centrepiece of her reflections.

Independence, mobility and dignity are things which most people take for granted until, at some point in their lives, one of them is dinted. When you are starting from scratch and you suddenly find that there is a way forward, there is hope and there is the possibility of living and working on equal terms, it is not surprising that you rejoice in the means to this wonderful end.

This is what Joyce does. Rejoice in the liberation brought by her dogs. I know how she feels and I commend this book to those who would like to share in her experiences and her success, in her profession, in her commitment to her local community and to the Guide Dogs for the Blind Association.

This is indeed a recollection of a full, fulfilling and giving life. I am pleased to have been invited to offer these few words as a preface to her book. I have one more dog and many more years to catch her up!

Her life's work, and her commemoration of this in the book speak for themselves.

Rt Hon David Blunkett MP

Prologue: Joyce Dudley - A Potted Biography

Only occasionally does the general public realise there is a hidden world of disability. This often occurs when a news story, or a person with a high profile, becomes centre stage for a while. Disability, the public then learns, comes in many guises and each form it takes presents the person concerned with immense challenges which need courage, resourcefulness and perseverance above the normal.

In the case of the blind community, made up as it is of many diverse groups and the guide dogs who have helped part of that community gain both independence and dignity, such a moment came when the Blair government appointed the Rt Hon David Blunkett, formerly the leader of Sheffield City Council, as Minister of Education. His guide dog, the only one in the House of Commons, made the public understand more fully than before how vital his companion was to many aspects of his life.

"By acting as a pair of eyes to enable a blind person to do a job, cross a busy street or a crowded railway concourse, a guide dog can take away some of the hurdles involved in getting from A to B, which any sighted person takes for granted," David Blunkett has written in his autobiography, *On A Clear Day*[1]. In his case his guide dogs have enabled him to live a fully public life both in Sheffield and in London.

Joyce Dudley is another person who has been able to live a public life, albeit on a smaller canvas. She is as well known in Wrexham as David Blunkett is in Sheffield. Like him, she too has lived among sighted people all her adult life and shown great

---

[1] *David Blunkett, On a Clear Day, an autobiography with Alex MacCormick, Michael O'Mara Books Ltd 1995, 9, Lion Yard, Tremadoc Road, London, SW4 7NQ.*

resolution and determination even down to the way she has organised her home and indeed lived in it on her own for many decades with a number of guide dogs for company and support.

Joyce was fortunate in her parents for both had striking personalities and were public spirited with an obvious concern for others. In the 1920's her father raised money for the War Memorial Hospital in Wrexham, finally built in 1926, by going round in a pony and trap, visiting the pubs, though he himself did not drink, to sell raffle tickets for the venture. Her mother, who was always engaged in voluntary work, especially for missionary and other causes, had a more personal stance and it is both her parents' attributes which have persisted in Joyce's outlook and the things she has done.

"Father always had it in the back of his mind that I must see as much as possible while I had my sight," Joyce has recalled. So she and her brother Eric, who left school at the height of the Great Depression in 1931/2 for a banking career, only interrupted by the Second World War, were taken to see many of London's historic places. These included Westminster Abbey, Horseguard's Parade, St James's Park and Buckingham Palace. They also had a boat trip down the Thames to the Tower of London. In 1935 they were in London again, for the Silver Jubilee of King George Vth and Queen Mary, this time standing on the Victoria Monument, where they watched not only members of the Royal Family pass by in their pageantry but also foreign heads of state, many of whom were later to come to unfortunate ends in the conflicts that were soon to rack Europe.

Joyce's education in Wrexham at Grove Park Grammar School also helped by giving her a grounding in intellectual life. She had a part in a production of St Joan and learned the Lord's Prayer and some grammar in Welsh, though it was not her forte.

iii

She was also a member of the Geographic and Scientific Society and once stood as a Conservative/National Liberal candidate in a mock election. Her leadership potential was recognised when she was made a prefect. In her teens she was still able to ride a bike and play hockey and tennis and for some years enjoyed ballroom dancing.

Ever since she can remember Joyce has loved nature. As a small girl she had never gone into the fields and woods without taking flowers home for her mother. She knew where the snowdrops grew and where to find primroses and harebells. If there were no flowers she would pick grasses instead. This sensitivity to the natural world has remained with Joyce and she still finds intense satisfaction in her garden. "I cannot literally see the beauties of nature," she has commented, "but I have a very vivid memory and now, using my hands, can create a picture in my mind's eye." She continues to attend classes at the Welsh College of Horticulture on borders, water features, the nurturing of lawns, flowers, trees and shrubs. "I've done practical work there, too," she has added, "including tree planting, pruning and hedge-cutting, as well as seeding and turfing a lawn." She has even done the homework which has been set to such a degree she has earned level one and two credits in the National Open College Network.

"I know exactly what the things I can touch are like," Joyce has commented, which has been of great assistance to her throughout her life. "My hands sing for me," she has reflected, "and were singing for me by the time I had guide dogs. What I felt with my hands could run straight up into my brain." Joyce has, too, a natural picture of objects, like the hinges on Notre Dame Cathedral in Paris, which she once visited. Her sense of touch, developed over the years because of her loss of sight, is paralleled by her hearing skills which have also been refined. She still knows what colours are like also and this helps her build up in her imagination the texture of the world around her.

Joyce's public life has of course mainly focussed on her job as a physiotherapist in a number of hospitals and latterly in her own private practice at home. But she has also taken part in local politics where she has represented her ward on the community council since 1986. In 1994 she became its chair person after a year as deputy. She enjoys listening and learning about a problem and trying to help solve it, where necessary taking the matter to the Council itself. She has now been appointed a Governor of a local infant's and junior school.

From April 1996 Joyce has served on the North East Wales Community Health Council and convened its Community Group. This has involved her in helping to monitor the work of the North Wales Health Authority, the local Hospital Trust and community hospitals. Through reports she has also learned about nursing and residential homes, speech therapy, chiropody and other specialist areas, all of which she has found absorbing. Other valuable aspects of her work have included visiting hospitals and nursing and residential homes and also attending conferences and workshops on topics as diverse as discharge from hospital and Cleft Lip and Palate services. Recently a North East Wales branch of Age Concern Cymru has been formed. Joyce played a major role in its establishment and is now a founder Trustee.

For nine years Joyce has visited the Day Centre at the Nightingale House Hospice, where she has made friends and listened and tried to give words of understanding and encouragement. She has also been a member of its Fund-raising committee, involving her in flag days, fairs and speaking engagements and has recently been appointed as a Trustee.

Her work in the uniformed branch of the Guide Movement from 1972 to 1982, first as a District, then a Divisional Commissioner has brought her more local prominence. This has continued through her membership of the Trefoil Guild, a section for non-uniformed members, which she chaired for four years. Her contact with the young members of the Guide Movement has continued to the present as from 1982 she has been a County Vice-President and from 1984 Wrexham Division's President.

When she attends functions, such as Christmas Carol Concerts, where members of the Association of all ages are present, Joyce refers to herself as "Guide Granny", as little ones would have no idea what a President is!

Joyce's enthusiastic support for the local branch of the Guide Dogs for the Blind Association has included chairing it for well over thirty years. She has spoken on its behalf to groups in schools and to the British Legion, Women's Institutes and Rotary among others. "You name it within a twenty mile radius and I've been there," she has commented. "I've got frozen, soaked and over-heated selling flags in the streets, collecting at supermarkets, helping on stalls at fêtes and bazaars." Now sitting on the music centre in her lounge is a replica of a labrador dog in harness on a plinth, one of the Guide Dogs for the Blind Association's national awards.

Underlying this activity has been a quiet but deep faith inherited from both her parents and appropriated by her, which includes nightly prayers. "I suppose I don't talk about it," Joyce has reflected, "but my faith has been a rock throughout my life." Her doctrinal convictions are straightforward - firm belief in God, and in Christ, who redeemed people through the cross and resurrection and brought eternal life. "I try, though often feebly," she has added, "to obey the commandments to love God and others as He commanded us." By preference and temperament Joyce prefers to make her witness in service rather than in obtrusive declarations so her faith is most revealed in what she does and how she does it, especially when people are in trouble or need. Like many others she misses the language of the 1662 Prayer Book and is less at ease with the Anglican revisions of it known as Series 1, 2, 3 or 4, but the church in Wales has its own revised version with which Joyce is now quite familiar.

Above all Joyce's determination to enjoy life is what is most characteristic of her, epitomised by her holidays when she will venture forth, either with friends, or with the Guide Dogs for the Blind Association tours, leaving her dog at home to be cared for by others. When she was younger she enjoyed sea and sun holidays in Spain, Portugal and Corfu, and latterly in Austria, Switzerland and Norway, where she and her friends have done much walking. More recently she has had holidays in Kenya and Costa Rica.

Joyce's visit to South Africa was perhaps her most adventurous holiday involving her flying alone with stops at Rome and Khartoum, where at midnight a hot, dry wind was blowing, then Nairobi and Salisbury (now Harare). One air hostess helped her at Heathrow when she left Britain, another at Johannesburg as she prepared to go through the necessary formalities on arrival. Having eventually met up with her friend Hilda Nield she spent her first weekend on the edge of Johannesburg in a beautiful house which had both a tennis court and a swimming pool as so many other white suburban houses there.

After two days and acclimatisation to Johannesburg's altitude, which she found difficult, Hilda and Joyce got into the Red Cross Land Rover Hilda used in her work and went to Swaziland, where they stayed in its capital, Mbabane. Soon they were lodged with two Dutch health professionals, friends of Hilda's, in their rondavel. Then began a month touring the country, including access to hospitals and a prison where mothers and their babies were held. One day Joyce's well-developed sense of touch was brought into play when she went out and picked oranges in the garden of two expatriate British farmers.

Joyce did not return immediately to London but had ten days in Nairobi with friends from her Wrexham life, who were working there for three years. Here she visited a rehabilitation centre for blind men and a boarding school for African children run by the Salvation Army, which she found very well equipped. Its head teacher explained to the pupils they had a visitor from England who like them was unable to see. Joyce was moved as they showed her how well they could read from Braille in English. Some she was told later hoped to enter one of the professions or become telephone operators, while others, suitably trained, would return to their villages.

Joyce was also invited to visit the King George VIth and Queen Elizabeth Hospital in Nairobi to talk to senior staff in the physiotherapy department from the point of view of a blind physiotherapist. She felt somewhat rusty as she had not been practising for over five years but as normal she used her formidable willpower to cope.

One lasting impression which fed Joyce's love of the natural world was a visit to a game reserve, where she and her friends came across two pride of lions amongst the many wild animals they spotted there, and a trip to the Rift Valley and its famous Silver Beck Hotel, where she had a drink with one foot in the southern hemisphere and the other in the northern.

When Joyce was working full-time she did not have the opportunity to pursue many of her later interests but did belong to the Talking Books library. She loved them so much they began to act as a drug and during the reading of *My Brother Jonathan* and *Adam Bede* she listened through the night so beautifully read were the chapters. Fortunately for her she likes to be methodical so it has not come hard to organise her house to take into account her disability, including keeping all doors either completely open or firmly shut. "In theory," she has remarked, "everything has a place and all is in its place. It works out pretty well but not always." She has, for example, opened a tin of fruit instead of soup and she does not always put things back in their proper place. She likes to do her own cooking, entertain friends and have visitors to stay. She does, however, never now cook chips because once the chip pan bubbled over. She uses a braille marked automatic washing machine and cooker controls, whilst occasionally utilising the services of a pressure cooker. Joyce still types on an old-fashioned dial typewriter and has mastered the phone.

Her guide dogs have always been free in Joyce's house and garden when appropriate, sleeping in their own bed in her bedroom and on a dog bed in the lounge, with special rugs for them in the dining-room and kitchen where they can relax and so Joyce does not fall over them. Her house has been cleaned for over twenty years by two married women who have kept her home clean and sparkling and never complained when there were many dog hairs to clear away during the moulting season.

One of Joyce's greatest pleasures is listening to the radio, normally Radio 4, which enables her to keep abreast of current and world affairs, and whose nature and science programmes she finds compelling. But she likes, too, Radio 3 and Classic FM, with a weekly concession to Radio 2 for its Sunday evening of popular music followed by Sunday Half Hour. For many years now she has attended concerts by the National Orchestra of Wales and the Hallé in Wrexham and they continue to nourish her spirit. In this way she has been able to live on a world map and among the sighted community as an equal. *Brian Frost*

Chapter 1

Going Blind

My parents were Londoners born and bred, my father Charles from Clapham and my mother Alice from nearby Battersea, though the Dudleys originally came from Kent and Surrey. There was also a continental connection for one of my grandfathers was of French origin. The Thames itself played a part in our history, too, because one of my grandfathers had been a barge builder on the river. He lived in a company house on the Isle of Dogs and it was here my father was born.

Both my parents were Christians, my father originally a Primitive Methodist, my mother Church of England. Before their marriage they would go on alternate Sundays to one or the other. After the marriage, however, my father was confirmed and became Vicar's warden, treasurer for a number of groups both religious and secular, as well a being master of ceremonies for charity dances.

My mother and father were good dancers, even winning a valeta competition which they had entered a few months after their wedding. Mother, like my father, was always involved in public work, either as Sunday School Superintendent, or collecting money on flag days for sundry charities. She could also be found in the back room making refreshments.

After their marriage in 1913 they went to Wales, to them a very strange country after London. For six months they lived in Caernarvon, where very few spoke English, and then moved to

1

Wrexham. My father was an auditor for the first National Insurance Scheme brought in by Lloyd George and it was here Eric and I were born, Eric in 1914 and myself in 1917.

My parents' experiences of life were quite different. My father, always the proud Londoner, took external courses for King's College and internal ones in the Civil Service itself in order to develop his career. During the First World War he was sent back from Wales to work in London in the Ministry of Munitions, before returning to Wrexham when the war ended. My mother, by contrast, had been through a secretarial school and become private secretary to the buyer for the Hudson Bay Company of Canada. My brother Eric and I were good friends, but we also fought, partly because he was a terrible tease. I used to get cross so out went my fist but I always came off the worse. My father used to urge me not to take any notice but I disregarded his advice and often lost my temper.

We were both confirmed when we were fourteen and involved in Scouts and Guides respectively, so we were brought up in an atmosphere of service to others. I remember thinking once, as I compared our family life to that of our peers, my parents seemed to have little time for the social round.

When I was five and had but recently started my education the doctor came to examine every pupil. My mother came to the school for the examination. I seemed a very healthy girl, he told us, then asked my mother if I had any problems? "I don't know that it's a real problem," my mother replied, "but Joyce doesn't look at things very straight. Her father won't have it and says she looks at things perfectly straight, but I don't think she does." "Oh," replied the doctor, "I'll have a look at her to make sure."

He asked the nurse to put some atropine drops in my eyes, then left me for about twenty minutes before starting his examination. He looked, then hesitated. "Have you put the atropine drops in this girl's eyes?" he enquired of the nurse. "Yes," she answered, so he asked for a new bottle. Putting the drops in himself this time he waited for twenty minutes, then had a further look. To his horror he found that my pupils had not dilated.

"H'mm," he commented, "your little girl seems to have some problems with her eyes, Mrs Dudley. I suggest you see a specialist as soon as possible." My mother was very upset and asked whom he suggested. "Well," the doctor responded, "there's a very good man from Liverpool, Dr Malcolm Stockdale. He is the child ophthalmic surgeon for the County of Caernarvon. I suggest your doctor makes arrangements for your daughter to see him."

At the time my father was away on audit in Caernarvon, as indeed was Dr Stockdale himself, who was in the county seeing children. Accordingly an appointment was made for me to go to Caernarvon with my mother, who would accompany my father and me when we saw Dr Stockdale. I knew she was very agitated and my father rather subdued, but at the time I did not understand the significance of this.

Dr Stockdale was very nice to me. I remember to this day I had to read letters from a sheet. At that stage I had not learned to do ABC but could only do Aa, Ba, Ca (phonetics) but I did what I was asked to do to the best of my ability. He had a very thorough look at my eyes, pressed on them and said "Right now, you run along to your Mummy. Your Daddy will be there in a few minutes." I went back to her and of course she wanted to know what had happened. She was very concerned when a lady hurried in, opened a cupboard and took out a bottle, then went next door again. Eventually my father rejoined us but he was very quiet.

We now went out for a meal together, afterwards returning to the hotel where my father was staying. I was left to play in the lounge while my parents disappeared into their bedroom. Here my father told my mother what Dr Stockdale had said : that I had infantile glaucoma and was likely to lose my sight altogether, at which point my father had fainted. My father also said Dr Stockdale had promised to treat me. I would need medicine and drops and regular visits to see him. I went home with my mother, who was now very depressed, and started on the medicine and drops. My father came home twice a week when he took me to see Dr Stockdale in Liverpool.

Looking back I realise what a tremendous sacrifice my parents made on my behalf. My father had a regular job but it was not highly paid. When he took out his treasury note case from his pocket and pulled out a pound note, then put his hand in his trouser pocket and took out a shilling, it was clear to me each visit cost a guinea. In addition there was the train fare to Liverpool for myself and my father twice a week to be paid. Clearly a large amount of the family income was being spent on me. Yet never once did I ever hear what it cost to keep taking me to Liverpool, or hear shortage of money discussed at all.

Another thing I discovered in later years was that my parents had decided they would tell no-one what the medical verdict had been, so I might not find out what could happen later. Meanwhile I had to wear glasses, which I disliked, especially when I was at school, where the little boys called me "Four eyes." When I went home and told my parents about this my

4

father said "Never mind. Wait till the school concert, where at Christmas you're a fairy, aren't you?" I said I was so he said "They won't call you "Four eyes" after they've seen you as a fairy, you wait and see." I had a lovely dress, trimmed all over with tinsel and a wand which my father had created. It was made of a long silver cane, with a silver star on top, and an electric light bulb in the middle, with a wire going down to a battery on the stem. The wand therefore lit up and when I went to the school concert I was the envy of all the other children. The boys never called me "Four eyes" after that. Instead they used to say "Oh, Joyce was the fairy, wasn't she?"

I used to go to Liverpool twice a week for three months. Progress seemed satisfactory, so my visits became weekly for a further three months. Then they became monthly, then once every three months so that by the time I was ten I went once in six months for a thorough check- up. I was of course short-sighted, but not very, so was allowed to sit at the front of the class. Apart from that my short-sightedness and my eye problems generally did not worry me at all.

When I was eleven I sat for the local scholarship examination which I passed. Accordingly I went to the Grove Park Grammar School in Wrexham where I thoroughly enjoyed myself, settling in well. But when I had just turned fourteen tragedy struck my great friend, Olwen, when we were coming home from school one late January day. We had got off the bus about three quarters of the way home and gone into a field. Then we had climbed through a fence and on to the railway bank. We were of course trespassing, but we had been there before and were behaving responsibly, looking for specimens for our botany lesson. We started on one side of the bank and decided that perhaps it was the less sunny side and we would be better elsewhere. So I clambered down the bank and over two sets of lines to reach the other side. Olwen said "I'll stay here a little while longer."

We went on looking and then Olwen said, "Oh, I think you're right and the other side is better. I'll come over." I had found a couple of things so went on looking, my eyes glued to the ground, having turned round and seen Olwen start down the bank. In three or four minutes I heard a train coming out of the nearby tunnel, which was quite close. Quickly I turned round again to make sure Olwen was at the back of me. But she wasn't there.

I looked and found she was lying against the far railway line. Dropping my school bags, I yelled "Olwen, Olwen, get up. There's a train coming." She didn't move. I ran down the bank, clambering over a set of nettles. I waved my arms and screamed "Stop! Stop!" But the train went mercilessly on. While it passed I hid my face in the bank, then when it had gone by went over to the far set of lines where Olwen was lying quite still, her left arm completely amputated.

She had been lying with her arm over the line and the train had gone over it. I seized her, moved her from where the accident had occurred back on to the bank. I thought "If I go for help she will wander back to the line." So I shook and shook her and eventually she regained consciousness. "If I go for some help, will you promise me you won't move?" I asked. "Don't leave me, don't leave me," she pleaded. So I said "All right you can come with me."

She yelled "I want my satchel, I want my satchel." I would willingly have left it there, but she was so insistent I picked up her satchel of books and somehow or other got her over two sets of railway lines, then up a bank, through a wire fence and across a field, to a garage. As we went across the field I pulled Olwen's gabardine over the dreadful injury as best I could. To this day I still know what hot, warm flesh feels like. "What's happened to my arm, what's happened to my arm?" Olwen cried out. "It's had a bad bang," I replied, "and it's gone numb. It's all right. We'll soon get it seen to and you'll be all right. Don't worry."

I half carried, half dragged, her across to a very high wire fence; then thought "I can't get her through there. I'll call for Mrs Lloyd. Oh, I'd better not tell Mrs Lloyd what's happened. She's got a bad heart, she'll have a heart attack." So when she came out I merely said, "Mrs Lloyd, will you go and ask Mr Voyce to come here quickly please. Tell him Joyce Dudley is in great trouble."

Immediately she went to find the garage owner who came running with two or three men. They leaped over the fence, took Olwen from me and gently took her off. The minute my responsibility was lifted from my shoulders I had hysterics but one of the men very sensibly slapped my face and brought me to my senses. "What happened, Joyce?" Hughie Voyce asked. I said "On the railway, Hughie." Soon the ambulance came and Olwen was put in it and we speeded to hospital. She was groaning terribly; then suddenly the groaning stopped. I could only think that the St John's Ambulance man with us had given her a whiff of something to ease her pain. In my anxiety I grabbed hold of him and shook him. "You've killed her, you've killed her, I know you've killed her," I shrieked, for I felt while she was groaning she was alive but when she was quiet I was sure she was dead.

We reached the hospital where Olwen was immediately taken to the operating theatre. Strangely she wasn't bleeding, for the weight of the train had sealed her arteries but she was severely shocked. The hospital wanted to keep me there, too, because I was also shocked, but I would not stay. "No," I said firmly, "I must go home." So off I went in an ambulance. I asked the driver, however, not to ring the bell near my house because my mother had flu and it would upset her. Moreover, when we reached my home I would not go in because I wanted to avoid upsetting her. News had already spread like wildfire and a friend of my mother's came out and said "Joyce, you'll come in with Auntie Betty, won't you?" I agreed so she took me in and put me to bed. Meanwhile my father went to collect Olwen's mother and take her to the hospital to be with her daughter.

It was a dreadful night. I could not get what had happened out of my mind. Then the police arrived. The policeman who questioned me was very nice but kept saying "But what happened, Joyce? Tell me exactly what happened. Why didn't Olwen get up when you turned round and saw her lying there and went over to her? Why didn't she get up?" "I don't know, I don't know," I replied, "she just didn't get up." He left it at that.

It was not until a fortnight later that the mystery of what had happened was resolved. I was visiting Olwen in hospital one day. She had not mentioned the accident at all during my visits but then suddenly said "Joyce, when you were on the railway line what hit me in the middle of the tummy making all the breath go out of me?" I said "Well, I don't know, Olwen, what hit you, but you fell." "But something hit me," she insisted. When I told the police about this conversation they said what had happened was this. After Olwen had come down the bank and reached the bottom she had caught her foot in the signal wire which had pitched her forward. She had then fallen on to the line on her solar plexus, which had winded her and made her curl up with her left arm over the line. That was how her arm had come to be amputated by the oncoming train.

I was away from school for two weeks after this accident; but Olwen was in hospital for weeks on end. She was a girl of marvellous spirit and had to cope with publicity about the accident which reached even the national newspapers. People sent all sorts of things to her and also to me. Olwen was in an upstairs ward of the hospital, which had a veranda. As it was near our school when we came out Olwen would come onto the veranda and pitch down oranges and sweets for us until the ward sister realised what was happening and chased Olwen back into her ward. Eventually she recovered, came back to school and did extremely well, though she was discriminated against because she had lost one arm when she went for an interview for the Civil Service.

At the time of the accident, and afterwards, I and my parents, too, I imagine, and certainly everyone else, thought I had come off very lightly. But when I went for my six-monthly check up Dr Stockdale found that the sight in my right eye was deteriorating. He therefore kept a careful eye on me and I had more treatment. Unfortunately he was unable to do any more and I lost the sight of my right eye within twelve months of the accident. But I still had quite good sight in my left eye. Soon I got used to turning my head round a bit more because I was unable to see in the right sector.

I took my matriculation examination a year late because of the trouble over Olwen's accident, passing in English literature and language, French, both written and oral, history, geography, maths and physiology, botany and cooking. Then I had a year in the lower sixth.

I was finding it difficult to make my up mind about the kind of job I wanted when I left the grammar school. I felt a little guilty about this because all my friends seemed to know exactly what they wanted. I knew the things I did not want to do but nothing positive had enthused me. Then one day I went back to the hospital where Olwen had been for a minor operation of my own.

I was there a week before coming home. "You're delighted to be out of hospital, I'm sure," my parents remarked. "It's nice to be home," I replied, "but I want to go back to hospital." "Go back to hospital?" they queried. "Yes," I told them, "that's where I want to work." Before I went in that week I had never considered working in a hospital; once there I knew immediately that was where I wanted to be.

I left school in July 1936 and that September went as a probationer nurse to the world-famous Orthopaedic Hospital in Oswestry in Shropshire, named after Robert Jones and Agnes Hunt, which was only about some fifteen miles from Wrexham. From its early beginnings my father had had dealings with the hospital and through his enthusiasm I had decided to apply to do orthopaedic nursing there. My course was to take two years after which I would either do general nursing or physiotherapy. On my first morning I was "Fitted" into my uniform, which was voluminous and not at all flattering. But the Home Sister explained "Come the winter you will need several layers of woollies under the dress to keep warm." And so it proved.

All the long wards were completely open which increased their coldness after autumn. I was allocated a young man's ward where I soon felt completely at ease and was very happy though initially I was rather shy. The work was very hard physically as most patients were either in heavy body plaster of paris or on metal and leather frames. These patients had to be lifted and turned daily by the staff to allow for adequate bodily care as they were immobilised sometimes for months, sometimes years, because of hip, spine or knee troubles. The food we were given was excellent and never have I worked so hard physically or been fitter.

After three months I went on to night duty on a young boy's ward whose ages varied from six to fourteen years. Mostly they were already asleep when I began my work, but I found it lonely as I was single-handed and also a big responsibility. Of course there was a duty Sister, who came round regularly and whom I could always ring, but it did not take away how hard I found it being responsible for all those children in that open ward. After Christmas I was transferred to the babies' ward, but was again single-handed, which I found even more stressful, partly because I had not been given a plan of the ward and the children had their names on their cots.

When I came off duty each morning and wrote up my report I could not see the lines on the paper in front of me. I informed the ward sister of this, who told me to report sick at the doctor's surgery. I went there immediately and explained what had happened. He wanted to know my previous medical history and indicated he would make arrangements for me to see an eye specialist in Shrewsbury. Matron, who also saw me, said she would take me off the ward and make me a runner who would go wherever one was needed; "but you won't have responsibility," she said firmly.

Within two days I went to Shrewsbury and saw an ophthalmic surgeon. Nursing was too great a strain and had an adverse effect on my remaining eye, he reported to Matron, and I needed rest and relaxation. When Matron and I discussed this I was so very sad. I kept thinking about my sight and its problems; about having to leave the hospital, where I had made friends and where I had been so happy. Matron was most understanding and urged me not to leave at once, "because," she said, "it will look as if you've been thrown out." There had been six probationers in my intake so she suggested I wait until we went on holiday and leave then. I therefore did another three weeks at the hospital as a runner before I left. It was spring 1937.

I now went to see my own specialist in Liverpool who agreed I must have at least six months rest with no stress involved before thinking about my future. This worked well for a week or two. I was still able to read and ride my bicycle, but I felt somewhat lost because my friends were away at college. Then I noticed that if I was under any pressure at all, made an effort to do something, or even became concerned about events, everything went misty. I would try to wipe away what seemed to be obscuring my vision in front of my eye.

Once again I went to Liverpool. Dr Stockdale, my specialist, was very serious about the situation and put me on further medication but as the weeks went on and the mists became more frequent it was decided in September I should have an operation. Sadly this accomplished nothing and I was left with only a little sight in the one eye.

Chapter 2

Lady

Had my eyes deteriorated in the last thirty-five or forty years I would have been sent to a rehabilitation centre. But in those days no such centre existed so I stayed at home with my parents, feeling rather lonely without my friends. It was a difficult time not only for me but also for my mother and father because I went through very, very dark days and my parents were the whipping boys. Moreover, they had had no experience of anyone losing their sight. Nor, indeed, had any of their or my friends. I lost belief in myself and my abilities and was a rather timid and reticent person so people did not know how to speak to me.

When my friends came home in vacations they were not so bad in their responses. After all they were also young. They accepted me as I was; but my parents' friends felt sorry for me and that was the last thing I needed. I had no confidence, no confidence at all and even if I went out to tea with my mother I was terrified I would spill my cup of tea or drop my cake. People would say "Mrs Dudley, would Joyce like another cup of tea?" as though I had no mind of my own. When I got home I would explode and say "They treat me like a fool. Because I can't see they seem to think I don't know if I want a cup of tea!"

So it went on. My parents were intensely patient. My father was especially wonderful and very keen for me to learn Braille. I had been a very good and quick reader and if I was unable to read, I equally clear I was not going to learn Braille to help me to read again. He was determined, however, and had another try. One day we went out for a walk and he said to my "Do you know what would give your mother and me more pleasure than anything else we can think of?" I said I didn't and he replied "If you were to learn Braille." I then said "Daddy..," but he quickly interjected before I could finish my sentence, saying : "I know you're not going to but I would just like you to know what pleasure it would give us."

This started eating away at me and eventually I capitulated and said "All right; I will learn Braille." I did not think it would ever be useful to me but I decided to please my parents because they were being so marvellous. I had a home teacher come every Wednesday morning and I learned the theory of Braille very quickly for after all I was young and not long out of school.The writing wasn't so bad but the reading - this I found most difficult because I had to learn to read by touch and I was not yet skilled in touch partly because I had only just lost my sight. I was not therefore a very good pupil. My teacher used to come at 10 a.m. in the morning and I would get my homework out about twenty minutes beforehand so little practise did I do. As a result I progressed only slowly but I did eventually become reasonably competent at writing with a hand frame, though reading really continued to be a struggle.

My parents were now looking to the future for me. They could see that my existence at home with them was no life. My father therefore made enquiries and found out the Royal National Institute for the Blind ran a physiotherapy training college in London. He thought it would be an ideal place for me because I had already been at an orthopaedic hospital. He sent for the college details and read them out to me. I was torn : half of me thought the prospectus sounded wonderful, the other half thought "Joyce, you can't do that, you wouldn't be able to manage." I was convinced they would not have me in any school.

So there the matter rested. I wanted to do physiotherapy but didn't feel I could. By this time Dr Stockdale had retired and recommended me to Dr Milnes Bryde in Manchester, whom I went to see regularly. He was most interested in my condition. Moreover he, too, could see it was no life for me being at home. One day he said "What are you doing now, Joyce?" I replied "I'm at home, Dr Bryde." "Well, what are you doing there?" he asked. I said I went to help weigh babies once a week.

Soon Dr Bryde made an appointment for my father to take me to the Royal National Institute for the Blind premises in Manchester. "What a pity you are not here next week," said the man who interviewed me there. "We have a visitor from London who knows all about physiotherapy at the College for the Blind."

I lifted my head very high, stuck my nose in the air and said "I'm very sorry. We've come from North Wales and I'm in Manchester today and not next week." I was not very polite. My father quickly capped my remark however. "Excuse me," he said, "if we could have an appointment for my daughter next week, I would willingly bring her." Accordingly an appointment was made but before we left I made it clear why I couldn't go to the college in London for an interview which might lead to my obtaining a place in the training college.

On my return visit I met a most helpful man who asked about my training and background. I discovered he was totally blind himself. He gave me the biggest telling off I have ever had. "Do you realise what a parasite you are?" he scolded. "Here you are at twenty-one and no more use in the world than a brown paper parcel. If you were to die tonight your parents might be upset for a month or two; but I'm not sure they wouldn't think after that it was just as well." He made me very angry indeed, just as he had intended and before I left him had agreed to go for that interview for a place in the college in London. It was the finest decision I ever made and after that I never looked back. I went to London for a month's probation in July 1939, passed the necessary examination and registered to start my training in September.

It was here I met Dick Pocock, the anatomy lecturer at the college, who was to have a formative impact on my whole life. He taught me not to be sorry for myself and that there were others in the world who had received more bitter blows than me. He pointed out, too, that I was young and had been given a good education. There was therefore a career waiting for me if I would make the effort to study. He also taught me to be aware of what was going on around me when I was feeling that my loss of sight was as though a bag had been hung over my head permanently. "Listen," he said, "it's amazing what your ears will tell you." I had been terrified I would not know the difference between a trolley bus and an ordinary bus but once I listened I began to hear the difference.

Dick Pocock in particular suggested I began to listen for the newsvendor on many a London corner and learn to be aware of the shop a few yards down the street on my way to the training school. "You'll soon smell it and know where you are," he considered. He taught me, too, to relate to different sounds in my surroundings. Hitherto there had been no-one who had the kind of knowledge he possessed to help me. Now through him I began on an upward path. In classes he would go round to each person and invite them to put their hands on a femur. Then would say "You can tell it's a right femur" and "You can tell it's a left femur" because of certain differences each had. "Feel it," he would urge so gradually I and my fellow students would learn to use our hands and convey what they felt to our brains.

My first four weeks at the school for blind physiotherapists transformed me as a person but because war had broken out on September 3 my parents were not at all keen for me to return to London as planned on 5 September. But by now I had got the bit between my teeth and I went back despite the outbreak of hostilities between Britain and Germany. Part of my training included work at St George's Hospital, then at Hyde Park Corner. Soon, however, I had to go to Epsom when the bombs began raining down on London and St George's moved. Now I was mixing easily with other young girls who could not see, some of whom had been born blind or had lost their sight later. Those who had been to college I often found to be very capable and I learned much from them.

During my time in London I had become bolder and learned how to change buses at Oxford Circus on my own. I used to ask as I stood by the bus stop "What number bus is this please?" and people would tell me. On Saturdays I would often go to Regent's Park where I was taught to row by an old Oxford blue, but the blitz changed all that challenging form of relaxation.

By 1941 I was ready to take my finals. That December we went to an air raid shelter in Great Portland Street in the basement of the headquarter offices of the Royal National Institute for the Blind and sat on wooden benches, with blankets over our legs to keep warm, for our examination. It included three hours of typing. Once the examination was over I went back to Wrexham and waited for the result. In due course to my great joy I heard I had qualified as a chartered physiotherapist. My parents naturally were equally thrilled.

In the spring of 1942 I started at the Emergency Hospital in Wrexham but I did not have my first guide dog to help me until 1950. I was one of a group of young staff who found pleasure in both our work and our play. We walked on the local hills, went to music concerts and several of us joined the recently formed branch of the Young Conservatives. I eventually chaired the local branch and began public speaking, something for which I found I had a natural gift. Twice I represented Wales in the London finals of the public speaking competition.

Several of my friends were in digs near my home so we went to the hospital together, my father, who was willing to run me anywhere, acting as chauffeur. Especially during my early years at the hospital I met patients, most of them injured in the war, who were full of courage and great fun to be with. They are imprinted on my mind for ever. One merchant navy officer from

Liverpool, whom we always called the Admiral, had been torpedoed in the Atlantic, spending hours in the water. Badly injured from his waist down, it was a long time before his fractures healed and he began to learn to walk again, for months in iron splints. He had a wonderful sense of humour, immense courage and on V.E. day instead of walking the long corridor still in his irons and with two walking sticks, went along with the sticks high over his head.

Then there was Alec, a young man of twenty-five and formerly in the RAF, who had been struck down with acute rheumatoid arthritis. He had already been in several hospitals before he came to Wrexham because it was near his home. When I first met him he had been unable to walk for months and was very low. We struck up a friendship and months after starting his treatment cheers went up in our department when he took his first hesitant steps. I have kept in touch with him since those days but sadly now he is in a nursing home after living alone and looking after himself for years. Twice a year, driving his adapted car, he used to come to visit me. Despite his pain and the immense effort it took merely to walk to my front door from his car, he was all smiles. With legs in irons and splints on his wrists he would say, chuckling, "I waddle just like a duck, Miss Dudley."

It was people like him and others like Raymond, a local Royal Welsh Fusilier, horribly burned in a tank hit by enemy fire, who made me count my blessings during the war. He arrived at the Emergency Hospital with legs healed but with horrific scarring. Attending our out-patients department daily for massage for over a year, he made slow but steady progress and was eventually discharged. I still meet him most Saturday mornings shopping in the supermarket.

One day two young officers arrived at the hospital from India. They had both caught polio while there and were paralysed from the waist down. Everything possible was done to help them but there was no improvement and eventually they were transferred to a special unit at Stoke Mandeville to be fitted with supports and splints to enable them to try and re-build their shattered lives. These two young officers and the Admiral were often guests for tea at my home on Sunday afternoon. My father used to collect them from the hospital and carry them into the house. Food was very strictly rationed then but friends and neighbours were very generous.

By 1945 having gained much experience I was promoted to a senior position. Two years later the Superintendent left and I applied for the post. At the interview I felt I did well when answering questions from the medical staff but the lay members of the panel were more interested in the fact that I was partially sighted than how efficient I would be if offered the job. The following day the surgeon in charge sent for me and informed me I had not been appointed it because it had been felt my lack of sight was too great a barrier.

I was heartbroken as I felt I was quite capable of being a successful head of department. I burst into tears and was very angry. I did not blame the committee but was greatly distressed they had been unwilling to give me the chance to prove myself. My father as ever was wise and pointed out that what I really loved was treating the patients and that had not altered. Moreover, being in charge would entail much more administration. I was in fact in charge for ten weeks after the superintendent left. This made me ask myself over and over again : "How can they refuse to appoint me because of my lack of sight, yet trust me for ten weeks as there was no-one else?" I felt the situation was most unfair but at least I had been able to prove myself during those weeks.

Events turned out very strangely. A senior physician, who had been on the selection committee, and had asked some very sensible questions, came into the department with back problems when I had been running it for a couple of weeks. He had physiotherapy for a fortnight and on his final visit asked me into his office. Thanking me for what I had done for him, he handed me a large box of expensive chocolates and said he had been very impressed by the way I had run the department. "I must congratulate you," he commented. They were golden words indeed, more than compensation for my disappointment.

In June 1949 after a short illness my father died following an operation for a benign brain tumour, the result of an accident twenty years earlier. I felt his loss deeply and at the time thought I would never even smile again, let alone laugh. In time I came to realise it was the best thing for my father as had he lived he would have been very handicapped and most probably an entirely different person from the marvellous man I had known and loved. By 1950 several of my friends had left the area, too, so I decided I would apply for a Guide Dog and that April went for training to the Leamington Spa Centre of the Guide Dogs for the Blind Association.

I was not entirely unfamiliar with dogs when I began to learn how to work and live with a Guide Dog having had two pets when I was a girl - a black-coated, curly retriever when I was ten, and an Airedale puppy when first at school. But naturally I had to start with basic principles and become accustomed to the fact that all guide dogs are trained to work on the left. I also had to get used to the stainless steel handle they have when in harness which is vitally necessary because, if you are unable to see and are to be guided, a wobbly item like a lead is of no use whatever.

I was soon taught to put on the harness of my dog, who was called Lady, and we started off. I was not at ease at all because here was a dog I had only just met and I had to hold on to her harness and follow her along the pavement. But it was made easier for me because Captain Liakhoff, my trainer, had a collar and lead on Lady so he could control her, an arrangement which continued for a day or two, after which they were taken off. By that time he was far from well so did not have many talks with his pupils but he was still brilliant with the dogs and very good at pairing them with suitable masters or mistresses.

We started by walking along a fairly straight pavement, just there and back, there and back, three times a day. Then we began going down side roads so that my dog sat at the down kerb and waited for my instruction "Forward." Then she would get up, proceed and cross the road. We did this also for a day or two, then learned how to go round right hand corners and then left hand corners. Next we learned how to turn back on ourselves and retrace our steps. Now we began doing more complicated routines. Up till now we had only crossed very quiet side roads but next we had to learn how to handle busier roads and how to work with our guide dog in traffic.

It is always the guide dog owner who decides which way to go and the dog which does the safe guiding. With the instructions "Forward," "Right," "Left," and "Back" you can manage any direction, wherever you want to go in fact, provided you know the area you are working. Besides these instructions

there are the commands "Sit," "Stay," "Down." When you come
to a road at every kerb you find your dog will sit. You then stand
there and listen, first right, then left. When you think it is safe
you cross, saying to your dog "Forward," which is a request, not
a command. If the way is clear and safe your dog will get up and
cross over the road. When it gets to the far side you say "Good
girl, my word you are a clever, good girl." The dog's tail wags
and she thinks "Aren't I clever, oh I do like my mum to praise
me."

But if there is much traffic and it is not possible to hear if it is
safe to cross - there may be a lorry near with an engine running
which is masking the rest of the traffic - you listen as best you
can, then say to your dog "Forward." If it is safe your dog goes;
but if it is not safe it stays sitting. You then say "Hup, hup, good
girl. When it's ready, mum wants to cross." You do not repeat
the request to go over for you have already made that earlier.
But you keep talking to your dog, keep its mind on the job and
when it is really safe it will get up and go. Once safe on the
other side of the road you again praise your dog, the only wages
a guide dog gets from its master or mistress. When you end your
walk and either reach home, or your planned destination, you put
the harness handle down and praise your dog again.

You were also taught at Leamington Spa how to care for your
dog, including how to give it a skin massage all over before
grooming, which is how you learn about any blemishes your dog
has. First you brush its hair the wrong way; then comb it; then
brush it again the right way. Dogs, you are instructed, should be
groomed every day and have healthy skins and coats, but
normally are not bathed. When they moult, then brush the coat
twice daily. Often I used a comb with twelve rubber teeth, which
is rectangular in shape, but two of my dogs, Tyler and Grant,

objected strongly to its use. Trainees are also given a health record book which contains the date of the dog's birth and its weight, among other details. It also indicates the maximum and minimum weight for your dog, which therefore has to be weighed regularly. This is more necessary with a new dog because of the stress it will lose weight to start with. When it has settled down once every three months is sufficient time for the checkup.

Eventually the day came for me to return home. By now I had learnt to step out and hold my head up as Captain Liakhoff had instructed me to do. I had learned, too, the amount of food I should prepare for each meal for my guide dog and that I should take it to the vet regularly to have it weighed. I was seen to the train and home I went to Wrexham with my Lady. I had a few days away from the hospital to settle Lady down in her new home and start her learning the way to the hospital. We did a little at a time so when I went back on duty Lady knew exactly where I wanted to go and that she wasn't going home for the day to stay with my mother. Rather she was staying with me in the physiotherapy department at the hospital, where a corner had been made available for her and a rug provided for her to sit on. Everyone I found was most interested in my guide dog.

Things did not run smoothly, however, partly I suppose because people then were not conversant with the Guide Dog Association's work, and the superintendent physiotherapist was adamant that Lady could not be there. "I am not having that dog in this department," he declared. I looked at him, not able to credit what he was saying. "But why?" I asked. "I am not having that dog in this department," he repeated. "She is scrupulously clean," I countered. "She won't be any trouble at all. You won't know she is here." "I'm not having that dog in this department," he said for the third time.

Had my father still been alive I would have turned to him for help and walked out of that particular hospital. But now I could not afford to act like this especially because of the family finances. I therefore stood there looking very forlorn and said "What am I to do?" He replied that Lady could stay for the day, but reiterated that she was not welcome in the department on a regular basis. So I took off Lady's harness and put her in the corner on the rug. "Be a good girl, darling," I said with tears in my voice. "Don't let me down." And she didn't. There was no sound from her all morning and following her run in the grounds after lunch there was no sound from her all afternoon either.

I was naturally terribly unhappy and worried so I rang up the secretary of the chief surgeon and asked for an interview with him next day, which was granted. When I met him I explained the problem, but the superintendent physiotherapist had already seen the surgeon ahead of me, who now told me how difficult the situation had become because "Your superintendent says he won't have the dog in the department, Miss Dudley." "Can I ask, sir, if he gave reason for this?" I enquired. "He was a man who was in the navy so easily could have lost his sight during the war." "I appreciate that," the chief surgeon answered "but it really is most difficult when he says he can't have the dog and you tell me it's necessary for the dog to be with you during the day."

"Do you think you could get a letter from the Guide Dogs Association explaining why the dog should be with you during the day?" he asked. "I'm sure I can," I replied, after which the surgeon said that if I did that he gave permission for Lady to be in the department for a month "while you are getting used to one another." "Thank you very much," I responded. The superintendent now never mentioned the dog and I didn't mention Lady, who kept a low profile while everybody held their breath. In due course the requisite letter came and I passed it on to the chief surgeon.

Lady stayed for a month, after which I was told that provision would be made for her to be kept outside the department. Every time a workman came anywhere near one of my colleagues would come and say "I hope he hasn't come to build a kennel for Lady." "Have they got any wood?" I'd ask. "No, I don't see any wood," was the reply. So another week would pass and no kennel came, then a further week. A month passed and still there was no kennel. In fact the kennel never came and Lady was never expelled from the department. But Lady, the superintendent and I - we all three never communicated. I communicated with Lady; I communicated with the superintendent and never fell out with him. And Lady stayed.

It was a long walk from my home to the hospital. It took me forty minutes and I had three busy roads to cross, but Lady did extremely well, never letting me down. It was such a relief to be able to get from home to hospital without any anxiety and with confidence, too. Formerly I had been struggling and hesitant, which had done something to the core of my personality, sapping my self-esteem. Now I had Lady I stood up straighter, held my head up and walked with confidence. Indeed, no more did I feel blind. In fact after I had walked with Lady for three or four months, and we had really got used to one another, I felt she was not guiding me but that we just walked along together. Before people had looked at me with my struggling hesitancy. Now no-one bothered to look for they had eyes only for my gorgeous Lady. This made all the difference and I regained the confidence I had before I lost my sight.

As I have already said Lady was a very handsome golden retriever, well proportioned with a lovely coat and splendid tail like a curtain when it was brushed out. But did she get dirty! It wasn't so bad if it was pouring down with rain, for there was enough to keep her clean even though she got wet. But when it rained and just stopped and the ground itself was wet when I arrived with Lady at the hospital her legs, tummy and tail, were full of drip from the road. It could not be wiped away easily but fortunately there was a low sink in the physiotherapy department and on bad mornings I used to go ten minutes earlier, put some lukewarm water in the sink and pick up Lady. Then I would put her in the water and literally wash her down. I did not have to wash her back, head and shoulders, but the rest of her I did wash down, then let the water out and dry her in the sink after which I would get her out and dry her again. For in no way could I have taken her into the department dirty in view of the past difficulties we had experienced.

In the early days when I had Lady dogs went to the Guide Dog's Association to be trained when they were already adult and their name given by their original owners, so there was no question of changing a dog's name. The pass rate was not particularly high because these dogs were adult and set in their ways before their training started. And some of their ways were not suitable for a guide dog. Lady herself had been trained as an adult, but she had done very well during her training. Nevertheless she brought with her when she came to live with me some of the tricks she had acquired during her growing up years. She was, for example, an awful thief and try as I would I never cured her of thieving. All I managed to do was to stop her actions by keeping things out of her way.

I would sometimes come home from the hospital in the evening and my mother would enquire: "Has Lady been all right today?" "Yes, perfectly all right," I would reply. "Why?" "Well there was a packet of bacon missing from the kitchen table after you'd left this morning." So a packet of bacon had been eaten I surmised. On another day half a loaf had gone missing and on another some butter. When my mother, who at that time did the shopping on her own, grew wise to this habit of Lady's she would put everything away so there was nothing to steal. Then by mistake she would leave something out and in a flash it had gone.

I remember once when I had been off sick for a few days and a friend had come to pick me up one morning. He took Lady and me to Oswestry and we went out for a cup of coffee and some beautiful home made cakes. I bought a chocolate cake and took it back to Wrexham. At tea-time I put it on the dining-room table and the dining-room was left for a couple of seconds by both my mother and myself. When we came to sit down my mother exclaimed "Oh!" "What's the matter?" I asked. "The chocolate cake's gone," she said. "It can't have done," I replied but she insisted it had. Sure enough there was a plate with only about three crumbs of cake left on it. In our absence Lady had put her feet on the table and woof! In a twinkling of an eye the cake had disappeared.

Another time Lady and I had gone to spend a weekend with friends who lived on a farm some five miles out of Wrexham. They invited my mother for Sunday lunch and their son went into town to collect the papers for my friend Mary, who had made a nice gateaux for pudding and piped it with cream. Somehow or other, while we were in the dining-room, Lady got into the kitchen. Nothing was missed at the time but the following Thursday morning, when I was getting up, and Lady was getting out of her bed, there was an "Oomph." "Hello, my girl," I thought, "are you being sick?"

I said to my mother "Will you look near Lady's bed, because I'm not sure whether she was sick or not this morning when she got up." Later that day my mother greeted me with "There was something very odd on the carpet near Lady's bed this morning when I looked." "What have you done with it?" I asked and was told my mother had wrapped it up in a piece of newspaper. I went and found the newspaper, got a bucket of water and some disinfectant, which I dropped into the bucket, stirring it with a stick. The I fished out - an icing bag! It had my friend Mary's name on it in marking ink, so there was no doubt where it came from. Lady, if you please, had got into the kitchen the previous Sunday where she had found the icing bag still with cream lying about on the kitchen table. She had just stood up to lick it when she heard someone coming, so had swallowed it entire. How it didn't kill her I never knew, but it had not.

In the days when I had Lady, and not many dogs were being used, the guide dogs were nearly all bitches so every six months they came into season. I knew very little about bitches and did wonder whether I would be able to use Lady to go to the hospital when she was in this state. I discovered, however, if I was meticulous about her toilet, I could manage. I would get up some quarter of an hour earlier each morning, sponge Lady down with some Dettol, or water, and off I would go.

I didn't often have trouble, but occasionally I would pick up a dog at the back of me. I could hear it there so would say to Lady, "Come on, girl, on you go, on you go." Then suddenly I would stop and bring up my left foot, which invariably caught the offending dog under its chin. It would yelp, then go running off. Later that day, before I left the hospital for home, I had to sponge Lady again, but with this care and the constant sponging I was able to use her right through her seasons. Indeed, she was very good indeed once in harness and would take no notice of any other dog.

But, my word, I had to be careful when she wasn't in harness. If I had not kept the gates at home firmly closed she would have been off. Guide dogs become Dr Jekylls and Mr Hydes really. When you put their harness on they are working animals and they will go through the motions they have been taught in the training school, which you continue when they come home. But once they are loose they are just well behaved pets who enjoy a free run and a romp as any other dog would. Guide dogs love their work but naturally it is not work for which they were originally made and so they have no inhibitions. Indeed, if they don't want to be guide dogs they don't respond. They must want to do the work and be willing to enjoy it as well for their training to be effective.

Lady was a wonderful guide dog for taking me to and from the hospital but I didn't do a great deal more with her. We had a good long walk there and back each day but very often I also went out in the evening with friends to places where it was not particularly easy to take Lady so in effect she became a hospital guide dog. But we got along well though when I went on one or two holidays I used to leave her with my mother at home.

Lady first came into my life in 1950 but by 1954 I realised as we went daily to the hospital she was not walking so quickly. By the time she was six I thought "Well, I suppose she is not as young as she was and does not want to walk as fast as she once did." I noticed this over a period of some two or three weeks. Then one morning to my horror she didn't eat her breakfast, which was most unusual. She was very fond of her food, especially when it was stolen. Now she wouldn't eat anything. I said to my mother that I must take her to the vet when I came home from the hospital, which I did. He examined her, but reassured me by saying he did not think there was anything much wrong with her. "I'll give you some medicine and we'll see how she goes," he concluded.

I took her home but she didn't eat any supper. She started on her medicine, but didn't eat breakfast the following day either. She now had eaten nothing for a day and a half so I felt I could not expect her to go with me to the hospital. That evening I came home and again found Lady would not eat, though she had taken the medicine during the day. Next day I asked my mother to ring the vet and ask him to come and see Lady, which my mother did. "Joyce is very anxious about Lady because she always eats her food so well," my mother told the vet. "She is terrified she is going to lose her." He said, "Oh no, no, nothing of the sort. Lady is not a very sick dog. I will give her an injection."

It was now three days since she had last eaten. The following morning she would not eat again but was sick when she got up. When I examined what she had brought up I was horrified. She had produced a piece of gauze and a syringe needle which she had obviously picked up in the hospital grounds. I was naturally appalled that such objects should be lying around the grounds and that Lady had found them. Now of course I thought she would be all right, so I left her at home and went off with my friends to work, yet still Lady did not eat.

Again I called the vet saying I was desperately worried about my dog. "If she had a piece of gauze and a syringe needle in her stomach no wonder she hasn't eaten," he re-assured me. "It would take a day or two to get over." Lady, however, became very lethargic so I rang up and got a day's leave from the hospital and took a taxi to see the vet. "Something has got to be done about this dog," I insisted. "She will die if something isn't done." "Just a minute," he responded and rang up the Liverpool veterinary college. They would see her as soon as I could get here there, he reported, so without stopping to get a lift from anybody a taxi was ordered, I got Lady into it, and we set off for Liverpool.

On arrival at the college we were met by a porter and Lady was able to walk in. Here I saw a splendid specialist who wanted to know Lady's history, which I gave him. I told him about the gauze and the syringe, but he didn't seem very interested. He asked me about her last season and said "I'll just take her into the surgery and examine her." He took her away and brought her back. "I'm very sorry to say that this dog has an acute inflammation of the uterus," he explained. "She must be operated upon. I will put her on a saline drip this morning and operate this afternoon."

I left Lady in Liverpool and went home. I rang up that night. Lady had had her operation, which involved a hysterectomy, and was being looked after all night. She was on a drip and receiving oxygen, with a qualified vet with her all the time. The specialist told me he would ring me at work the following morning, which he did. "I'm very sorry, Miss Dudley," he said, "Lady died at three o'clock this morning."

I was completely shattered. I was particularly upset because I felt crucial time had been lost. It may have made no difference had I gone earlier to Liverpool, I will never know, but I remained convinced much time had been lost. The result was that my darling Lady had died when perhaps she need not have done. The whole hospital was upset, too. It seemed as though a member of staff had gone, for everybody knew Lady by now.

In due course her death certificate was forwarded to me which I sent on to the Guide Dog Association, who were also very sad at what had transpired. They assured me that as soon as there was a suitable replacement for me they would recall me for training with a new dog.

Chapter 3

Shandy

Roughly half way through February, 1956, one very snowy morning my mother saw me off at Wrexham station for another journey to the Guide Dog Training Centre at Leamington Spa. It was still overcast when I arrived and the staff were very busy clearing the snow away because, though we could not go into the town itself until the pavements were cleared, we could start our initial training in the grounds.

Things had changed at the Training Centre during the five

years that I'd had Lady and I learned that no longer did the dogs go back to their kennels each night. Rather they stayed with you in your bedroom. Two students shared a room and I shared mine with a pleasant girl from Scotland called Mary. We quickly became friends and when I had been there for a day and a half I was introduced to my new guide dog, Shandy. She was lovely, a pure Labrador. Consequently I thought she was very short coated compared with my beautiful Lady. She was not quite as big, but a very nicely proportioned dog, aptly named Shandy I was told because the main part of her body was lemonade coloured. Her ears were darker, too, like beer, so really she was a beer-lemonade shandy girl.

I had a new member of staff, Eric Hatchley, whom I had not met before. He was a nice young man from Devon, with a great sense of humour and a lovely Devonshire roll in his voice. We related extremely well and after stressful sessions we used to repair to the local pub where Eric would regale us with stories about Devon. The next day Shandy and I did some work together in the grounds so we could get used to the feel of one another, working under Eric. When bedtime came I took Shandy down for her run before we went to bed. "Now these dogs are going to be very excited coming to live in the house," Mr Hatchley explained. "They have been living in kennels for five or six months so before you go to bed, or before you leave your dog in your bedroom, please see all your possessions are put either in the big cupboard or in the drawers."

When Mary and I undressed we carefully did as instructed and when we took our housecoats and slippers off, they were put away, too. The floors were polished and immediately Mary's dog jumped up on to her bed. She got her off a couple of times and then we settled each dog down by our respective beds and clambered in. Mary's dog, Penny, was her first guide dog so she was excited and thrilled. "I'll let Penny sleep on the bed tonight," she said. "She'll have to go down on a rug tomorrow and when she gets home she'll have a dog bed. I'll soon get her into the habit of it."

My little one curled up by my bed as I said "There's a good girl. Night, night Shandy. See you in the morning." All was quiet. I waited a minute or two and then a paw came up on my bed. "Get down on your rug, there's a good girl," I said. I waited again. First one, then another paw came up. "Get down on your rug where you sleep please," I said firmly, "there's a good girl". I waited again. First one, then another paw came up. "Get down on your rug please," I repeated firmly, "where you sleep. Be a good girl and go to sleep for the night."

Once again I settled myself down. "Ah," I thought, "Shandy's gone to sleep this time." But not a bit of it. After five minutes up came her paws again. I said sternly "I'm still awake, young lady.You get down on your rug, there's a good girl." Down Shandy got. I thought to myself "This battle has to be won tonight because, if I don't win it now, I've had it. But she's not sleeping on my bed." I liked Shandy, loved her already, but I did not want her on my bed. So I kept watch and the little monkey waited now for perhaps ten minutes then first one paw, then another, came onto my bed. "I'm still awake," I said. So down Shandy went yet again.

I waited for a further twenty to twenty-five minutes. I thought she must be asleep now but suddenly she put two paws on the bed and heaved her body up on to it, lying as still as she could, doubtless thinking "My mum won't know I'm here." I said "But mum does know you're there, so come along off this bed, my lady." I stayed awake till 2 o'clock that night keeping Shandy on the floor. In the end she did get down and there was an almighty sigh. She went "Woof" and I was then allowed to go to sleep. When I woke up in the morning she was still on her rug. After that I did not have any problems again and Shandy never once tried to get back on my bed. This was very good because Penny slept on Mary's bed the entire three weeks we were at the Leamington Spa Centre.

Once the snow had been cleared from the town we started our work in the streets. It was more comprehensive than the training I had received before. We did more varied routes, for example, and we went into a store, on a bus and walked along a canal. We were getting on very comfortably together but unfortunately one day when we were out walking late in the afternoon a fishmonger came out with a long pole and pulled down his metal shop front just as we were passing. His action startled Shandy very much indeed and she was upset. Indeed, her work went to pieces that day.

My trainer saw immediately what had happened and said "Right, stop her and take her harness off. Bend down, reassure her, give her a big hug and come along back in the student's van." This we did. The following morning we went out together again but Shandy was still very nervous and apprehensive and was not working well at all. We struggled the entire morning and again in the afternoon. During supper Mr Hatchley said "Miss Dudley, I would rather like us to have a walk this evening." I looked at him and said "You're anxious about Shandy, aren't you?" "I want us to go out this evening," he explained, "where it would be very quiet and there would be nothing to upset Shandy at all. We've got to get her confidence back and reassure her." So we went out walking that evening and for a couple of days I did not undergo the same training as the rest of my class. Instead Shandy and I went for very quiet walks until she regained her confidence, which fortunately she did.

When I'd had Shandy for about ten or twelve days we went to bed one night, I said "Goodnight" to her and she curled up on the rug by the side of my bed and I went off to sleep. I woke up next morning and said "Hello, young lady," as usual, then got my bedroom slippers out from under my pillow. Putting my feet out of bed I thought "Oh dear, what have I put my feet in?" It did not feel like anything nasty, nor did it have a smell. I had a look and there on the rug was a great pile of thick threads. I could not think what on earth it could be. Fishing round further I found pieces of material. Examining them I said "Mary, did you put your things in the drawer and cupboards when you went to bed last night?" "I'm afraid I didn't," she answered. "I left them on the chair at the side of the bed." "Are they there now?" I asked. She looked. "No," she replied, "they've all gone."

Evidently during the night Miss Shandy had gone across and taken Mary's pants, petticoat and bra and nibbled down every seam. Hence the pile of material all in pieces on the rug which were the seams of her garments. I did not know exactly what the procedure was, whether I should give Shandy a whacking, tell her off verbally, or what. So I said, "You wait here, young lady, and I'll go and have a word with our trainer." Picking up a handful of stuff I went along to Eric Hatchley's room and banged on the door. "I'm very sorry to disturb you, Mr Hatchley," I said, "but I wonder if I could have some advice." He came out and asked what I had in my hand. "They were Mary's undies when she went to bed last night," I explained, "but I'm afraid Shandy took them to pieces in the night. What is the procedure? Do I rub her nose in them and give her a good telling off?"

"No," he replied, "just gather them up, put them in a waste paper basket, take Shandy down for breakfast and for her toilet, and I'll deal with Mary at breakfast time. It isn't the dog's fault, it's Mary's fault for not doing as she was told." I went back to our shared room and was very contrite about what had happened. "Oh, Mary, I'm so sorry," I said. "I'll see if we can go into town today and replace your things." "Don't worry," Mary responded, "I've got plenty of things here. It was my fault for not putting my clothes away." At breakfast time Eric Hatchley said to us all "We make our rules for a very good reason. If you follow them this sort of thing doesn't happen. You must think always whether your actions are going to affect your dog," he added. "I told you they would all be excited. Shandy had a wonderful time last night taking undies to pieces."

At the end of three very happy weeks I said "Goodbye" to my fellow students and to the staff and was seen on to the train at Leamington Spa station. When Shandy and I reached Wrexham my mother was there to meet us both. I introduced Shandy to her and they responded well to each other from the minute they met. We had no problems because there was a dog bed in my bedroom and Shandy was very happy to sleep there. I now had a further few days holiday and during that time I did with Shandy, as I had done with Lady - I taught her the way to the hospital. I knew, of course, where I had to go: straight, forward over a road, where I had to turn left, then right, and on to the hospital's physiotherapy department. This I now taught Shandy. Then a couple of days before I was to go back on duty, I introduced Shandy to my colleagues and showed her where she was to lie. By this time the department had moved into new premises and she had a bed in a corner. I introduced her to this and the following Monday off we went to start hospital life together.

Then my problems began. From my first meeting with Shandy in Leamington Spa to the time she had come home she had been my constant companion. She had been either out in harness, working, or on a collar and lead in the training centre. At home, too, she was with me but on the loose. In each of these places all had therefore gone well. When on my first morning back, however, I reached the physiotherapy department and took Shandy's harness, collar and lead off, sat her on her bed and went to the staff cloakroom to take off my own coat, I looked down only to find she was at my heels. I immediately took her back to her bed, settled her down and returned to the staff room. It was no use: there was Shandy in the staff room with me again.

I thought to myself "I must fasten her until she gets used to staying on her bed while I treat my patients." Accordingly I took her back and fastened her to her bed. All was well while she could see me. She remained on her bed, quiet as a mouse, but in those days there was no open department, only one which was curtained. There were both male and female sessions, and mixed sessions also, but all three were treated in curtained cubicles. As soon as I disappeared into one of these with my next patient Shandy started to cry. She cried and cried and cried in a tone which was a mixture of whining and heaving. I quickly went to her, reassured her and gave her a cuddle. "Mum's only a few yards away," I explained, trying to calm her insecurity, perhaps the result of having had three homes - with her original owner, then in the kennels at the training centre, and finally with me. "If you listen you'll hear mum's voice."

Once again as long as Shandy could see me all was well but the minute I was out of sight she began to cry. I was very concerned. Clearly the superintendent, already none to keen to have Shandy in his department, would make a very valid point about not having a guide dog which cried to distract the patients. Moreover Shandy's crying was making it very difficult for me to concentrate on my work. Lunchtime came and all was well again. We had our lunch together, I took her for a run in the grounds but as soon as the afternoon sessions started and I disappeared from view Shandy began crying once more. By the time five o'clock came that evening I was worn out both with work and worry. Shandy had not slept for a single minute. Yet she still worked well on the way home. When she had been there for about fifteen minutes I fed her and immediately after that she flopped down and spent the rest of the evening and the whole of the night asleep.

I now contacted the staff at Leamington Spa and told them what had transpired. They said I was doing all I could to reassure Shandy and that she would get used to the routine. Eventually this proved to be the case, but it took about three weeks before Shandy really settled down and was prepared to tolerate me out of her sight. It wasn't an easy time for her and it certainly wasn't an easy time for me.

Then came my turn for weekend duty, which in the first instance consisted of treating patients in the physiotherapy department on Saturday morning. That was easy, because by now Shandy was used to my disappearing behind curtains. But weekend duty also entailed ward work on a Sunday morning. I got to the hospital one Sunday with Shandy and settled her on her bed, giving her one of her toys to keep her company. I fastened her, told her to be a good girl and that I'd be back, then off I went.

I had been on the ward about three quarters of an hour when a message came from the ward sister to tell me Shandy was jumping up at the window of the physiotherapy department. Back I went to find Shandy in a terrible state. She was really agitated, covered in perspiration and panting. Moreover she had chewed through her leather lead. I felt really silly for I should not have fastened her with it but I had not come across her problem before and not foreseen what might happen. Clearly she had chewed it through in order to jump up at the window. Now was no time for recriminations so I settled her down again and finished my work but I was very worried about what to do.

The physiotherapy department was always cleaned very well at the weekend. So I thought I would see the domestics who cleaned the floors because I got on very well with them. I asked them if it would be possible when I was on weekend duty for them to clean the floors on Sunday morning so Shandy was not left alone. It would be no problem at all they responded. So that is what happened. Now and again I bought them presents, perhaps a box of chocolates or some cigarettes. The plan worked well and while the cleaners were in the building Shandy remained calm.

All the time I had Shandy leaving her alone was a problem. In those days adult dogs were trained as guide dogs as I have indicated and were not prepared for the life they were going to lead so a few found it somewhat dehumanised from the life they had led as puppies. Shandy never grew out of this and remained devastated if I was out of her sight. I could take her with me anywhere, she would curl up on little more than a sixpence and you would never know she was there.

She didn't even mind how many hours she waited for me and would even go to a symphony concert, or a political meeting, and you would never be aware of her presence. She even behaved well in a car, but once I left it and was out of sight for a second she would start going "Woof! Woof! Woof!" which she continued until I came back into view. It became a big worry and a distinct disadvantage, yet she was a real pet. She adored me and I her. Lady, of course, had been fond of me, but Shandy went one better - all she wanted was to be with me, near me and to please me. Indeed, she worked extremely well apart from this defect and I was thrilled with her.

I had returned home from Leamington Spa with Shandy in March, 1955, and in January, 1956, out of the blue, late one night my mother had a severe stroke. I called the doctor and a specialist was also called such was the concern. I rang up the hospital and obtained special leave. My brother Eric and his wife came up from Sussex, where they then lived, and my sister-in-law, Iris, stayed for a month and ran the house. I remained at home to look after my mother as it became obvious that though she partially recovered from her stroke she could never again be responsible for the home.

Much talking and soul-searching went on about what to do. I had applied for extended unpaid leave from the hospital where I was still a senior physiotherapist and thought I would be able to manage. However, my brother was doubtful about my ability to run a home which I had never done before, as well as look after my mother. "Eric, I know my capabilities and weaknesses," I told him. "Just let me see if I can do it. I shall soon know if I cannot carry out all I should. But I can only help mum if she is downstairs, so I can keep an ear on everything during the day."

Beds were accordingly brought into one of the downstairs rooms and Eric and Iris returned home. It was an anxious time for me, looking after a sick person when I hadn't any sight. I remember, novice that I was, burning two panfulls of carrots before I realised how much water you had to put into a saucepan in order to boil them so they did not run dry. It was a very difficult life for Shandy, too, after being used to going each day with me to the hospital.

While Iris had been with us I had been able to go out with Shandy for a walk each day. But once she left my mother was not so keen on being left alone. I thought wryly to myself "Now I have a dog who doesn't like being left and a mum who doesn't like being left either." However, after being with her all day, one evening I said "You will be perfectly all right if I go out. I shall only be out about ten minutes, but Shandy must have a walk. Be good till I come back." "Don't leave me, don't leave me, please Joyce," my mother pleaded. "I'm sorry, mum," I replied, "I have been up since 6.30 this morning and looked after you all day. You are perfectly all right. Shandy has been waiting, waiting, waiting. She must now have her walk." I put Shandy's harness on and off I went. I ran round the streets. Indeed, I could not get round fast enough because I was so anxious about my mother. Of course when I returned I found she had been perfectly all right. Nevertheless she made a fuss for the next couple of evenings when I again went out with Shandy. But after that she never complained about my going out with Shandy and leaving her. She was so good when she realised that she was safe.

I was now no longer at the hospital treating patients and at home I had a different challenge. Fortunately I was a physiotherapist so knew what to do. We used to arrange physiotherapy for my mother three times a day. I had a tray of all sorts of things that she had to use to manipulate her affected hand and I also started to give her leg exercises. Gradually I got her to her feet and walking with a stick. I also taught her to dress herself except for the corsets, which she could never manage. Nor for that matter could I!

Some four months after her stroke, when my brother and his wife came to stay for a few days, we were able to take my mother's bed upstairs again because by this time I had taught her how to go upstairs and come down backwards very carefully. She was naturally absolutely delighted with her progress and that she was able to be a little more independent. I would give her a duster and she would do the dusting. I also put things ready and let her lay the table, which for her was a mammoth mountain to climb.

Shandy's life by now had changed much. Now we were the shoppers so we would go into Wrexham three times a week. I had someone come in and help with the housework and while she was there Shandy and I would shop. We had to find out where the fish, meat and electricity shops were and also where we could buy bread, cakes and buns. This took a little time but in four or five weeks we could find our way to all the places in Wrexham we needed to visit. Shandy was extremely good at shopping and learned to know the difference between the shops. We would go down a street and I would listen to see if I could hear the delivery van for the bread, or smell it. Once near the shop I would say "Shandy, bread;" then "Good girl," when she found the shop. I would go again three days later and use my sense of smell and say once more "Shandy, bread." We would go through the shop door and when she had found her way to the counter I'd say "Clever girl." After five or six times when I said "Shandy, bread" she would go to the right shop straight away.

Shandy had thoughts of her own. She couldn't see why, when we went to the Manweb shop, where I paid the electricity bill, there was any sense in standing at the back of the queue.

We used to go in through the door and I would say "Hup, hup," and Shandy would move forward carefully. I thought to myself "H'mm, I think I know what is happening here." But I merely said "Good girl, move on" and then "Stop." When I reached the counter I realised there had been a waiting queue and would say "I'm so sorry, I'm afraid we've jumped the queue." "That's all right, dear," would come the reply. "You go in front of me." So I would pay the bill and off we went, leaving the rest of the people in the queue still waiting!

One day a visit proved absolutely hilarious. I was going into W.H. Smith's some four or five days before Christmas. It was only a small shop in those days and I thought "I guess it will be jolly crowded in there." So I opened the shop door and said "Hup, hup, take care, take care, there's a good girl, it will be crowded." Shandy moved forward very carefully as I thought to myself "We must be by the counter now." "Hup, hup, good girl," I repeated. Shandy moved on and on and then seemed to round a corner before sitting down. I said to myself "There's something wrong here," for I could sense it. Then I realised what Shandy had done. "Shandy, we are on the wrong side of the counter," I explained to her, so back we went.

Then someone put a hand on my shoulder and said "Hello, I'm the manager." "Hello," I answered. "I've been watching your dog," he went on, "she's absolutely wonderful. I saw you coming through the door and thought you needed help because the shop is very crowded. But you spoke to her, she looked round the shop and moved very carefully forward, avoiding all the people. She then went round the end of the counter and as far as she could go as if to say 'Now you'll be able to get served at the front'."

Another day when I was in town I came along a side street,

past the General Post Office and needed to cross the road. I got Shandy to find the kerb and said "Forward." She moved forward carefully. We were about half way across the road when suddenly I lost my hat. It was in the days when tall hats were fashionable and I was rather smartly dressed to go into Wrexham. I stopped Shandy and kicked a little with my feet but couldn't find my hat. So I got Shandy back onto the pavement and waited for a pitter, patter, pitter, patter, which would indicate another pedestrian was level with me.

"I wonder if you would be kind enough to pick up my hat for me," I said. "There you are, dear," said the lady who had picked it up. I said "Thank you very much," but sensed she had not moved on. I put my hat back on, moved forward again and dropped my head a little, so I did not lose the hat again. I then heard the lady who had helped me say "It was the ladder on top of the van." Apparently a GPO van had been parked in the street, with ladders protruding from its top and as I had come at the back of the van a ladder had caught my hat and sent it flying.

Guide dog bitches were still entire then so I still had to cope with Shandy in season as I had with Lady. But by now veterinary Amplex had come onto the market so I used to give it to her during her three week season. I gave her two pills last thing at night, though soon realised this was insufficient, even though I also gave her another first thing in the morning. So I would put a pill out on her bed and put the alarm on for 3.30 a.m. When it went off I would crawl out of bed very slowly, pick up the pill, find a very sleepy head and open Shandy's mouth. I popped in the pill and closed her mouth. She would gulp and then down went the pill, down went her head and I got back into bed myself. I did not have to do this very often but it was a great help, even though we were both a very sleepy pair in the middle of the night. I used the same procedure as I had before when sponging her down with a solution of Dettol before I took her out. Once again if I picked up a dog I would stop Shandy, give the offending animal trailing us a clip under its chin with my foot, and off it went.

Once my mother had recovered enough to move about the house and go up and down to the toilet I was able to have a Saturday off every three or four weeks. I had a neighbour who lived nearby who kindly came to be with her. She also got lunch and tea as well as keeping my mother company while Shandy and I went off to Cheshire for the day. I used to get up very early and prepare everything before we left and make sure my mother was dressed before Mrs Longhurst came. It was about a twenty-five minute walk to catch the bus for Nantwich where I spent the day with my friend Hilda. Shandy enjoyed it as much as I did, partly no doubt because my friend had a dog with whom Shandy became great friends. She was also able to have a couple of wonderful runs on the nearby hills and also in the woods.

Hilda and her sister Mary kindly invited my mother and myself to stay with them for Christmas and New Year three years running. It was wonderful to have this holiday in 1956, 1957 and 1958 as well. It gave me a welcome break from running the home. Shandy had a whale of a time with Rupert. Shandy, of course, was a dog who had been trained to work mainly on pavements in residential areas and in Wrexham that is what we normally did. But when we went to stay with my friends at Christmas we were out in the country. Mary therefore suggested I take Shandy out on the nearby hill in harness on my own. "I think, Mary, probably we will get lost," I suggested," but Mary retorted "Go on, I'm sure you will be all right. Take a stick to help you."

I was not sure whether she thought I wouldn't be safe but she sounded so confident I thought to myself "Here goes." So I put Shandy's harness on, grabbed a stick and went off. To start with I had some idea of the way to go, but when we reached the top of the hill there were so many ways to select I felt completely and utterly lost. Shandy went on and I went with her, trying to keep my faculties alert and decide where we were. Suddenly I heard a pumping station and thought "I'm sure now I know where I am. Good girl, Shandy. Now go and find Rupert." Shandy got me back perfectly. I did not actually know where we had been but Shandy did and she took me back across the hill to Mill House where I was staying. I gave her tremendous praise and hugs so much so that she thought she had been a clever girl, as indeed she had. Certainly I thought she had been brilliant, though how she did it I still don't know. After that we had many walks together on the hill and Shandy also had free runs as well, which was only fair. Here I found peace and tranquillity and grew to love the birds, the feel of the bracken underfoot, the atmosphere of the seasons and the aura of the earth.

Shortly on our return from Cheshire after our 1958 Christmas and New Year break my mother had another severe stroke which affected her other side. Sadly she did not recover this time. She was never again able to stand or walk and needed a tremendous amount of care and attention. I had by now become used to running the house and managed to give her the help she needed. Knowing I had no sight I did not want to risk not being aware of any deterioration that might occur so I arranged for a district nurse to come in and give my mother a blanket bath once a week. This would ensure a competent professional eye was kept on my mother which reassured me, too.

Once again Shandy had to take second place to start with as

outings were cut down and we did not even go out shopping. We did manage a little run for her in the evening for ten or fifteen minutes but eventually we were able to get back to the routine we had worked out. Now Shandy was shopping once more and getting her proper outings. My mother, however, continued to deteriorate and for the last three months of her life the Little Sisters of the Assumption, whom my doctor had suggested I contact, came twice a day to help her.

The Little Sisters were splendid. I myself am a Protestant and the Little Sisters Roman Catholics. I had never before had anything to do with Catholic nuns whom I imagined to be very holy, serious and straight-laced. They were nothing of the kind I discovered. Indeed, they turned out to be most delightful ladies, wonderful with my mother. I suppose they had been coming for a fortnight when one of them said to me "Joyce, would it be all right if I said a little prayer with your mother before I leave?" "Sister," I replied, "I am sure my mother would be delighted." So we three had a prayer together which my mother thoroughly appreciated. Some ten days later a sister who did not normally come arrived and when she was saying her goodbye to my mother heard her say "But, sister, you haven't said a prayer." My thanks still go out to them for all the care and love they gave my mother during the last few months of her life.

In January, 1961, one Saturday night after midnight my mother slipped away. Naturally I was very sad to lose her but glad to see her at peace. She had experienced a very hard five years and had been so patient in her trials. In the end she wasn't the mother I had known and I recognised the time had come for her to find her rest. It could not have been easy to suffer for that length of time yet in a way I have always felt she gave those five years to me. Had she died when she had her first stroke I might have been very tempted to give up the home, go into digs and be looked after. But having run a home for five years and looked after my mother taught me how to keep a house running when I was on my own. So I shall be forever grateful for those five years which prepared me to stand on my own feet in my own home I hope for the rest of my life.

Naturally at the end of my mother's life I was very run down indeed, exhausted and tired. Before I could even think of starting physiotherapy again I realised I had to get myself really fit. I therefore resolved to stay at home for a few more weeks, then visit Surrey where my brother and sister-in-law now lived for a week or so before taking up my career again.

Before these plans came into operation my friend Hilda, who was then a Red Cross Field Officer in Southern Africa, in the three High Commission Territories of Basutoland, Swaziland and Bechuanaland, wrote to say she thought I should have a good holiday. She suggested that if I would fly out to Johannesburg on my own she would meet me there and I could then spend a month in the southern African sun. I wrote back immediately to say I was delighted and set wheels in motion to make this trip possible.

I had the necessary injections and made the arrangements for my flight to Johannesburg, then went to Surrey with Shandy to stay with Eric and Iris. I also went for a weekend to stay with Dick Pocock, my former tutor, and his wife, with whom I had first stayed when I went to London to do my physiotherapy training, leaving Shandy with my brother and his wife. It was lovely to see them again after such a long time and we greatly enjoyed our weekend together. When I returned to my brother's I found that Shandy had been quite happy with them so I had no fears over leaving her with them when I went on my southern African holiday.

My brother and his wife took me and Shandy to Heathrow to catch my plane only to find the flight had been cancelled until at least the next morning because of a structural defect. However, I was able to catch another plane two hours later than my scheduled one, though inevitably I would arrive late. I was assured a message would be sent to my friend in Johannesburg about the late change in arrangements so I said farewell to Eric and Iris and my darling Shandy and went with an air hostess to board my plane.

Thus began for me a new experience for I had only flown to other parts of Europe before. First we came down in Rome and later in Nairobi. I came off the plane with another air hostess but Hilda was nowhere to be found and no announcement over the loud speakers elicited any response. She had, it transpired, gone to the airport early, then heard my initial plane was cancelled, so had left, not having received the message to say I was arriving on another, but later, flight. She had been back at a cousin's house but ten minutes when the airport rang to say I had arrived. So, re-united with Hilda, I began a thrilling few weeks in both southern Africa and also in Kenya with some friends I had known in Wrexham. Shandy and I were apart but because I knew she was in safe hands I did not worry about her or, to be honest, miss her for she was but one part of my life, albeit an important part and now I was enjoying another aspect of my life's journey - travel.

Chapter 4

More of Shandy

When I left Africa for England my brother, his wife and Shandy, too, were at Heathrow to greet me. Shandy did not know what to do with herself to show her pleasure at being with me again. She had been a good dog while I was away and Iris reported the only problem had been that she would not be left alone! I sympathised with her because I knew that at times it would not have been easy to deal with Shandy's anxiety.

I stayed two or three days with them and then Shandy and I left for Wrexham. I returned home a totally different person. I had gone to southern Africa worn out and not very confident. Now after six wonderful weeks away, two of them in Kenya, I was fit, well and full of confidence, ready to start a new chapter in my life.

I had given it great thought. I really did not want to return to my former hospital. I had been in a senior position when I left but obviously my post had been filled. That was fair enough. There was a post for me as a junior but, though I did not mind being in that role when I began my career, I did not think that after some fifteen years at the hospital I wanted to return to a junior post. I wanted more responsibility and a challenge not less, so I decided to try and get part-time work at another hospital and begin a private practice.

A great friend of mine who lived next door to me came in a couple of mornings after I'd settled back home to tell me there was an advertisement in the local paper for a part-time physiotherapist at the War Memorial Hospital. I applied and was invited for an interview. Shandy and I set off after I had given her a splendid groom and made her look nice. I had also taken great care with my own appearance and made sure I arrived at the hospital in plenty of time.

I was given a very thorough and fair interview. "Well, you know you have offered us three mornings a week," they said. "But you have also told us you are hoping to start in a private practice. How long might you be with us?" I said I would give my word that if appointed, however busy I became with my private work, I would still come to the hospital three mornings a week because I loved hospital life and the work there would be so different from my private practice. "I feel it would keep me up to date and that I can learn much from my fellow physiotherapists," I added. To my joy I was appointed.

The next Monday Shandy and I set off for the hospital. I wondered how Shandy would behave in the department. I need not have worried. We reached the hospital, found our way up to the staff room, changed and then I made my way to the physiotherapy section. It was, to my great relief, an open department, with no curtains in evidence at all. A friend had taken Shandy's bed to the hospital the previous week so I settled her comfortably on it and said "Stay there, be a good girl, you'll be able to see and hear your mum the whole morning." I had a pleasant physiotherapist, older than me, with whom I worked for a few weeks and soon I was back into a routine. I grew conversant with the way this particular department was run and was soon finding my way round. Shandy was as happy as a sandboy. When I went to the staff room for my coffee I popped her harness on and she took me there and back. Then I would put her harness back on her bed and get on with my work, re-harnessing her at the end of each morning as we left for home.

My mother had left the family house to me which was as well for I had not earned any more money for five years. I decided to sell it and buy something more modern. The house in fact was too big for me on my own and if I were to use it for physiotherapy I would have to see that it was re-wired. Moreover, since my mother had died, it no longer seemed home to me and its significance seemed to fade. I therefore asked my friend next door to look in the local papers and soon was consulting an estate agent about a possible property in the same area. We went to see one bungalow but though it was new I was not very impressed with its layout. But as we went towards it we saw a small, semi-detached house which was also for sale. "Who's selling it, it wasn't advertised in the paper," I commented. Obviously, my friend indicated, it was being sold privately because in the window was a notice "This house is for sale - apply within."

I hadn't really thought of buying a house that was not brand new I explained but my friend persuaded me to look at it as it had not been built very long ago. So we went up to the front door, rang the bell and were met by a lady who invited us in and showed us into the lounge. "Would you sit down for a minute or two, because I'm just changing my little girl's dress," she said. While the lady, Mrs Davies, went upstairs, my friend told me what the lounge looked like. "Would you like to look round?" Mrs Davies enquired when she returned. This we did, I enquired about the price and asked if it were negotiable. "My husband may be prepared to drop it a £100," she replied. "But I must warn you the house will not become vacant until September." "That would suit me fine if I decided to buy," I responded, "as I have a house to sell." We then left and I told her I would let her know my final judgement.

I was quite impressed with the house and also excited but not finally convinced I ought to buy this particular property. Then I remembered a friend knew another local resident who lived in a similar house to the one which interested me. She allowed me to wander round this house with more leisure than I had before which clinched the matter for me. Accordingly I rang up the estate agent handling the sale and bought Mrs Davies' house. Soon my brother and sister-in-law were with me and they, too, visited the property which they also liked.

I did, however, need to consider how Shandy would settle down in a new home. There was no side gate by the garage, for example, to prevent Shandy getting from the back garden into the front, which I did not want in case she went into the street. So a gate was needed. I also needed a solid driveway before I moved in and a run for Shandy. Fortunately there was a suitable area bordered by the back of the storeroom, the coalshed and one side of the garage, which could take a run. I would be able to have a drain put in the middle, on the main sewerage and a tap also supplied, a solution which was ideal.

I now put my own house on the market. It proved less difficult to sell than I had imagined, which pleased me as I did not relish the thought of showing numerous people round my home. As it happened a buyer soon appeared. As Mrs Davies had been so kind to me I tried to be kind to the buyer, letting the re-decorating start before I had even left. The day after the Davies' family moved out of their house I had it decorated from top to bottom. The drive and the run were also completed and a side gate erected.

When the removal men came a friend had Shandy for the day. By the end of it, with the help of another friend, the beds were made up so by the evening things were very straight. Next day Eric and Iris came for the weekend which enabled Eric to do many small things for me. They left on the Sunday night and the following morning I went to the hospital as usual. But when I came home that afternoon I was lost. I had no patients because I had yet to start the private practice, and everything in the home had been completed.

The following day I went into town and had coffee with friends but again when I returned in the afternoon I felt lost. By Wednesday I had called at some other friends on the way home so I was not back till three, but things still seemed unsettled. I was miserable on both the Thursday and the Friday and became convinced I had done the wrong thing in moving. Nevertheless I decided to have a house-warming on the Saturday which kept me pre-occupied. Friends came on the Saturday evening, one let a saucepan of milk boil over on the new cooker and others dropped crumbs on the floor so by the time they went my house was no longer merely a house but my home. After that I never looked back. Shandy, too, who had been with me on one occasion when I viewed my future home, settled well. By the time she had been there three or four times all I needed to say was "Come home with me" and she would know where to go.

I now set about building up my private practice. I obtained a treatment couch and a short wave machine, as well as other equipment. I was not allowed to advertise, it was against professional rules then, so I made local doctors aware of my existence. One afternoon, though I had my confidence and knew my capabilities, I still wondered if I would ever have any patients. I suppose I doubted if they would be willing to trust themselves alone to a blind physiotherapist, for in the hospital they knew if they were not satisfied, or fearful, there were others who they could seek both for advice and help. Knowing how little money now lay behind me I thought "What shall I do?"

It was clear the answer lay in returning to hospital to work full-time if the worst came to the worst; but I need not have worried for the business did take off, partly because I was known locally to many people. Very soon I had all the work I needed. Some of the local doctors were extremely helpful and my own doctor in particular backed me to the hilt. It was, I discovered, more lonely in private practice for I had no companions to share responses with. Moreover, whereas the patients I saw at the hospital were younger and a greater challenge, at home it was older people who came to seek my help, some of them old "country characters." But I came to know them more personally than was possible at the hospital so there were advantages and disadvantages to both aspects of my professional life.

What was I to do with Shandy I asked myself because of her inability to be on her own? I decided she would have to become part of the practice itself. In fact she very quickly became the unofficial receptionist. When the doorbell went and I went to the door, Shandy came, too. I opened the door and said "Good afternoon," took the patient's coat and hung it in the cloakroom, while Shandy pottered upstairs, as we followed. When I opened the door of the treatment room Shandy walked in, straight into her corner and curled herself into a ball. You never knew she was there, whether patients were with me half an hour or longer. As soon as a patient was fully dressed and ready to leave Shandy rose up from her corner and tried to open the door. She then went downstairs and stood by the front door to see the patient out and waited for the next arrival. Every patient I had she saw up to the treatment room and down from it.

One morning when I was on duty at the hospital I heard Shandy shaking her head several times. "She must need her ears looking at," I thought. "I must take her to the vet and get him to clean them." Then as the morning wore on I was not so sure. "Those ears sound very funny," I said to myself. Lunchtime came, I put her harness on, and Shandy and I returned home. I popped her into her run and she then came in. I was getting ready for my afternoon patients when she shook and shook and shook. "Come here, Shandy," I urged, "let mum look at those ears." I almost had a fit when I did. Both ears felt like a golfball, swollen and hard. "What on earth's wrong?" I asked myself.

After the disappointment with the Wrexham vet over Lady I had been recommended to another one in Chester, who I now rang and asked him to see Shandy. "Bring her as soon as you can get here," he said. I waited for my first patient to arrive, then explained the situation. "Don't worry, you attend to your dog. I'll come on the next date agreed," was the reply. A friend I rang immediately brought a car and off we went to Chester. "How long has Shandy been like this?" the vet asked. I explained the history. "What has she had to eat today?" he continued. "Raw egg and milk this morning and some meat," I answered. "That's it," he exclaimed. I looked at him in disbelief. "She has eaten raw eggs ever since I first had her," I told him. "She's got an allergy to eggs," he replied. "Just a second, I must examine her chest."

The vet put a stethoscope to her chest, went to his medicine box and got out a syringe. He then gave Shandy an injection and me some tablets for her to take later. "It's a blessing you brought this dog immediately," he told me. "If you had left it until the evening surgery, she would have been dead." "Dead!" I exclaimed. "Yes," he said. "She has fluid on her lungs." "But why..," I began. "The egg was perfectly all right. It was fresh. It wasn't stale in any way." "She has suddenly got an allergy to eggs," he explained. "Surely at the hospital you have met patients who have worked with flowers a long time yet suddenly get dermatitis?" "That's perfectly true," I responded. "You give Shandy those tablets," the vet concluded. "She had an injection and she'll be all right now. But she must never eat another egg or anything which has egg in it in the future." Poor Shandy! She was a very sick dog for forty-eight hours but then was fine after that.

Shandy and I had moved into our new house in 1961. By 1965 she was twelve years old and certainly beginning to age. She was still working extremely well but twelve years for a Labrador is quite old. She had naturally slowed down and indeed was becoming an old lady. As the months went by it became clear she was not as fit as she should be so I took her to Chester again to see my vet, Mr Lambert, who thoroughly examined her and said he thought she had uterus trouble. "Oh dear, shades of Lady again," I thought as Mr Lambert put Shandy on a course of antibiotics. She picked up for two or three weeks under his treatment; but then went down again so back to Chester we went.

Shandy was given more antibiotics but within another three days she was very sick and a nasty discharge had started. Again we went to Chester to see Mr Lambert who examined her once more and said he did not know what he was going to do. "I thought this was going to happen. If there is any chance of her continuing I must operate," he told me. "Quite honestly, she has turned twelve, she's toxic and I don't think she will even stand the anaesthetic." "Something must be done," he added, "so I will try."

He said he would not keep Shandy that day but that I was to take her home, get as much fluid as possible down her over the next twenty-four hours, and glucose, too. "Bring her in at ten o'clock tomorrow morning," he requested. "May I ask you one favour?" I responded. "May I come along with Shandy when you operate, because she gets very upset when she is away from me and I would not want her upset before her operation." "Yes, you may come in," Mr Lambert replied, "but you do realise she may die." "I do," I answered, "but I promise I will not make any fuss, or distract you in any way at all." "All right, off you go. See you at 10 o'clock in the morning," Mr Lambert said finally.

My friend had sent his car and driver to Chester and I got him to stop off on the way back to Wrexham so I could buy three pints of milk from a diary and a box of glucose from a chemist. Once home I made up dishes of milk and glucose. To start with Shandy thought it good and readily lapped it up. But then she seemed to be saying she did not want any more. "Now you drink that and be a good girl," I said. "Do it to please me." By persuasion and exhortation I managed to get her to drink three pints of milk and most of the glucose during that day. Next morning off I went to Chester, feeling very sleepy because I had undergone a sleepless night.

Mr Lambert took us in saying "We are going in on a wing and a prayer." To start with he shaved her but gave me a clear indication he did not hold out much hope that Shandy would stand the anaesthetic. "So far, so good," he commented. "Yes, she's anaesthetised. We might be lucky." I sat on a stool at the end of the operating theatre and Mr Lambert explained to me every move he made during the operation. He did not cut Shandy down the middle of her stomach. Rather he cut down the side of her loin. When he got inside and started to remove the fibroids of her uterus he exclaimed "I can't believe what I'm getting out. It's absolutely fantastic."

Right, I'm stitching the outer skin now," he indicated, adding "She's a tough old thing. I would never have believed Shandy could have stood this." Finishing what he was doing, he went up to her head and told me "She's just starting to come round. Come, feel the bottom jaw. There's just a bit of weight in it." Sure enough there was. "Now I'm going to do something you may think very strange," he commented. "I'm going to put Shandy outside on a cold corridor because I want her to shiver. Once I've got her shivering, then she will be tucked up nice and warm." Turning to me he said "I don't suppose you've had any breakfast. You go off now and have a cup of coffee and lunch and come back at half past two."

A friend from Chester had come to the vets during the operation and we went into town for a drink. We wandered round one or two shops, then had lunch and arrived back at 2.30. I went in to see Shandy, who was lying down on a blanket in a warm room with a lamp near her. Mr Lambert pronounced himself well satisfied with her condition and said I could call and collect Shandy at 6.30 that evening. My friend brought us home and I prepared Shandy a bed in the kitchen. I put down a mackintosh sheet, then newspapers and some blankets, then put a clean sheet on the top in a warm corner of the kitchen. We returned to Chester for 6.30. Mr Lambert carried Shandy into the car and put her on the back of the Traveller on a sheet. Once home my friend Fred and I picked up the sheet and transferred Shandy to the kitchen. I covered her with a blanket and she seemed very peaceful and quiet, breathing steadily.

I now made myself supper and some friends arrived to see how Shandy and I were. After they went into what had by now become a teeming wet night Shandy grew very restless indeed. She was breathing badly and I grew most concerned. Mr Lambert had said if I was worried I was to ring him which I did about 11.15. "Don't worry, I'll come," he said, which he did, despite the flooding he had to negotiate to reach me. He gave Shandy an injection and said : "We'll just hope she will be all right now. It is going to be a very anxious night for you, but we can do no more."

I left Shandy covered with a blanket and thought "I'll get the sun lounger in." I put it in the kitchen and went to fetch an eiderdown from upstairs, leaving the door from the kitchen into the hall open. I grabbed it and a pillow, tore off some clothes and put on a housecoat, and started downstairs. Suddenly I stopped. I could smell disinfectant. "Oh no," I said to myself. "She can't have moved." Dropping my eiderdown and pillow, I crept down the stairs a step at a time. When I reached the bottom there she was. Shandy had thought I'd gone to bed without her. She had reached the start of the stairs and collapsed, her head on the bottom step. I burst into tears; then gently put her on the bed, settled her down and put the blanket over her. I prepared my own bed and kept watch all night. Needless to say I did not sleep at all.

In the morning Mr Lambert arrived but prior to that Shandy had struggled to her feet and made for the back door. "Oh, don't worry about going out to your run," I said. "Mum's made a special bed. Please just spend a penny there, darling." "I don't do things like that," Shandy indicated. "Out to my run I must go." So I put her collar and lead on and gently led her outside and held her up. She spent a great big penny and I helped her in again just before she flopped down on her bed once more.

Mr Lambert came to see her and was reasonably pleased with her condition but said she ought to have some fluid and food. What had I got? "I've got a pound of best mince," I told him. "Cooked?" he asked. "Yes, cooked." "Put out a small portion and warm it so there is an aroma and see if you can get Shandy to eat," he suggested. "Unless anything untoward happens I'll leave anything further until tomorrow."

I could not manage to get Shandy to eat that morning at all but I did persuade her to drink some warm milk. But by the afternoon, after I had warmed some mince and put a little in her dish, she was willing to eat. It was the start of her recovery. By next day she could walk around the ground floor, get into the lounge and on her bed there. She could reach her run, too. She now began to lap up all the food I gave her - the best mince; grated cheese; a tin of sardines, then some special dog food. She needed to because after her operation she was so weak and thin. As days went by she ate more and gained strength. Mr Lambert told me her wound would swell but that I was not to worry. It certainly did but then began to subside.

Twelve days after her operation I took Shandy to Chester and her stitches were removed. "Well," Mr Lambert said, "I think we have done as much as is possible. Shandy is looking better than she has looked for a long time." Now she just progressed and progressed so within three months had grown all her coat again. Indeed it was not even possible to see where she had been operated on. Now when she was free running she was actually galloping. I never thought I would see her do this yet even though she was now twelve and a half her speed was tremendous.

These were really the early days of the Guide Dogs for the Blind Association. Things had not much developed from when I first had Lady and there was no aftercare as today, when every twelve months one of its qualified staff pays a visit to see how you and your dog work together. When your dog is ten there is an aftercare visit every six months to establish if your dog is still working well and it is not too much strain for the animal. Had there been aftercare in 1965 Shandy may well have been judged ready for retirement but now she continued to work with me, though I cut down her work as much as possible. I had a friend whose daughter was on the hospital staff and as she lived near me I used to go to her house each morning with Shandy in harness, then take her harness off and take her to the hospital on her lead.

Shandy and I were going on quietly together when I realised another problem was rearing its head. Shandy was losing her hearing. If she were in the lounge and I was in the kitchen when I called there was no response. If I went into the lounge she sensed my presence and came immediately. I knew there was nothing that could be done about her hearing so became extra careful when we crossed roads together. There was, of course, no comparison between the volume of traffic then and now but even so if I was in doubt I put her handle down and asked for sighted assistance.

Twelve months after Shandy's operation she began juddering her jaws. So off I went to Chester again for Mr Lambert to see her. "She's got a very bad tooth," he reported, "with toothache. There's nothing for it but to remove it because antibiotics are not going to cure it." "How we are going to give her another anaesthetic I do not know," he continued. "Mr Lambert," I replied, "Shandy is not a young dog anymore. She is very precious to me, but I cannot have her suffer. If you try and take her tooth out and she doesn't recover then so it must be. I cannot have her with toothache." So she was given more fluid and glucose and went off to have her tooth removed.

Naturally I was again with her as she was put on the operating table. Indeed, I had my hand on her. As she began to react to the anaesthetic she stopped breathing. I held my breath. Mr Lambert gave her an injection, then some heart massage. The suspense was appalling. My hands, now resting on the side of the operating couch, would not stop shaking. I waited and waited, then Mr Lambert said, "One, two, three, four, she's breathing. We've pulled her back." He opened Shandy's jaws, took out the bad tooth, swabbed out the gum and very quickly she came out from under the anaesthetic. The tooth extraction was nothing like her major operation so I was able to take her out to the car and home. She was so happy in a few days time because her toothache had gone.

Our life together continued, rather low key. I had still got my beautiful, lovely, old Shandy and she was working a little, too. Now, however, her back legs were starting to go. I knew therefore the day must soon be coming when I would have to part with her. I was in Wrexham one morning with her and on the way home Shandy walked me into a ladder, something she had never in her life with me done before. As we came home I thought about it and came to the conclusion she was now not seeing as well as she should have been. I waited a couple of days then thought "Come one, you're being a coward. You just face up to things." So I rang up and made an appointment to see Mr Lambert.

By now I also knew Shandy had gone stone deaf. Mr Lambert took one look at her and said "I'm sorry, Miss Dudley, Shandy's almost blind. Her sight will go very, very quickly. Her legs are going, too." "Yes, I know they are," I admitted. "Well, what?" he enquired. "Mr Lambert, I'll have to part with Shandy," I confessed. "I'm afraid you will," came his reply. "I can't leave Shandy today," I added. "I'll make some arrangements and bring her back here in two days time."

I came home with Shandy for the last time, had a word with my friend in Cheshire who said "If you'd like to bring Shandy we'll bury her just outside my garden." Here there was a field in which Shandy had often run in her younger days so we agreed to do this. Arrangements were accordingly made for my driver and the estate car to take us to Chester. I was on duty in the morning but I did not tell anyone in the hospital what was to happen that afternoon because I knew I would break down, which I did not want to do. I came home quietly, then went off to Chester with Shandy. I cuddled her before Mr Lambert gave her an injection in her front leg. Shandy went gently down on the couch after which her gave her a big injection in her heart. Then he carried her out, put her in the estate car and we went off. Hilda met our car with a wheelbarrow and we picked up Shandy and lay her in it. The driver left us and I spent the rest of the day with Hilda.

We trundled Shandy through her garden and laid her to rest in the field as we had agreed earlier. I put Shandy's harness with her because I felt that was what had bonded Shandy and me together for all those wonderful years.

Chapter 5

Lippe and Mandy

Shandy died in the middle of May 1967. An aunt of mine, of whom I was very fond, came to stay with me for the next week which helped enormously. The day after she left I went to Surrey to spend a week with my brother and his wife which again was healing. I then returned home to set about the difficult task of preparing to open my heart to a new dog.

It is very difficult when you have been with a dog, as I had

Shandy to let her go and get ready to welcome a successor but in the middle of July I heard from the Guide Dog Training Centre at Bolton they had a suitable dog for me. Both Lady and Shandy had been trained at the Leamington Spa Centre but by now a north-west centre had been opened in Bolton so I went there for my three week period of training.

The centre had been purpose built and was fine for both students and dogs. Each student had his or her own room with a dog bed in it. I worked with my trainer Ken for two days, learning foot and arm movements and voice control, then two days later met my new guide. She was a big Labrador bitch called Lippe. Now Lippe was spayed. Both Lady and Shandy had been entire; but by the time I had Lippe the policy of the Guide Dog Association was to spay bitches after their first season when they went into training and to neuter their dogs after about seven months, while they were still being puppy-walked.

Lippe and I settled down reasonably well together but I found her so different from Shandy. Shandy was warm and loving and so close to me. Lippe was a big, handsome, laid back girl, who seemed to indicate she would take much winning. I tried extremely hard while I was at the training centre not only to work well with Lippe but to win her heart and affection. But I did not feel I was succeeding. Commonsense, however, told me "You had Shandy all those years, you cannot hope to start with a new dog where you left off with the old. It will inevitably take time, patience and perseverance, all of which you must put into this partnership." At the end of the time, which had gone relatively smoothly, we passed our final test and I returned home with Lippe. She settled very quickly into my home but was still somewhat distant and hard to win. At times she would play and we would have a great time but when the game ended she said

"Right, that's it, mum. I'll just go and sit on my bed on my rug."

We began working in the Wrexham area and I taught Lippe the way to the hospital. I had two or three days off after my return home and was not tired when I started back on duty yet things were anything but easy. In the morning, for example, when I harnessed Lippe and went out, she dawdled every step of the way to work. Yet she was a young and large dog who could move along well if she wanted to. I discovered that when I went into the town when I approached its busier outskirts Lippe would lift up her head and tail and step out most beautifully. Evidently we were beginning to get somewhere. But when we started for home once we approached the residential streets she would drop her head and tail and dawdle, dawdle, dawdle.

Reluctantly I got in touch with the Bolton training centre and they gave me some advice. Now one of the things you are told in training is never to feed your guide dog immediately you reach home because it will realise home means food and start pulling. So I thought to myself let me see what I can do with Miss Lippe and some food. One morning when we started out for the hospital I took out three or four Spiller's shapes, showed them to Lippe, then said "When we get to the hospital, Lippe, you shall have the biscuits."

I put them in my pocket and off we went. We dawdled every step of the way. When we reached the staff room I gave Lippe the biscuits as promised, and told her what a good girl she was. I took her out in the late afternoon, before her evening meal, and said "Have your tea when you get home," but it was to no avail. I also took her for some long walks and when she was on unfamiliar ground she did extremely well. Yet she continued to be less successful in the residential areas which surrounded my home. Try as I would I could not get her to work at a reasonable pace. I was still then young and wanted to be up and moving so found her dawdling very trying. Moreover I did not feel a bond was being formed between us either, even though Lippe seemed to accept me.

I had kept in touch with the training centre where Derek Carver, the Regional Controller for the Guide Dog Association , understood students' problems as well as being superb with the dogs. In October I rang him up and told him things were not improving. "I'm sorry, Miss Dudley," he sympathised. "Tell me honestly, Lippe herself, food and you: where do you come in that trio?" "I come third, I'm afraid, Mr Carver," I responded. "You've made a great effort these past three months," he conceded, "but obviously you have not succeeded. I'm afraid the only thing is for Lippe to come back to the centre and for you to have another dog."

I felt an absolute and complete failure. "No, don't feel like that please," he counselled. "Most of our matches go smoothly and are fine. But occasionally one does not. I'm afraid this is something you will have to accept." I therefore made preparations to have further time off from the hospital, packed my things and went back to the Bolton Training Centre. I arrived there feeling very down indeed and also upset and sad. The car taking me drew up and before I realised it the back door was opened and one of the kennel staff took Lippe away. I got out of the passenger seat at the front as two of the trainers I had previously met when I was with Lippe came out and gave me a wonderful welcome. "Lovely to see you again," they exclaimed. Then, each putting an arm round my shoulder, they walked with me to the centre itself. "I'm delighted to see you back," one of them said. "I've got trouble with my knee after playing football. I shall need some physiotherapy." They will never know what they did for me that day.

One of the trainers who had come to greet me had a dog for me called Mandy. She was a Labrador, smaller than Lippe, about the same size as Shandy but darker. Mandy turned out to be so different from either Lady, Shandy or Lippe. She was a right little modern Miss, full of life and pranks, always smiling and tail wagging. If I ever had to be cross with her over anything and even scold her she seemed to say "All right, mum, if it's got it off your chest, that's OK by me, but it doesn't touch me." I trained her very successfully and brought her home. She settled down quickly and we started a very good partnership indeed.

All guide dogs are trained principally on pavements, because this is the place where normally dogs and their owners work. But there are also dogs who work in the country without many pavements. This is a somewhat specialised training and all guide dogs get a certain amount of it so Mandy was no different. But though she had received no extra training as I was soon to discover she was outstanding in the countryside. We used to go on Saturday and Sunday when I had more free time for a host of country walks. Of course it was never easy without pavements to know where the turnings are yet Mandy learned very quickly and became highly skilled.

Guide dogs must have a free run on a regular basis. When they are in harness they are on duty, have to be responsible and concentrate. But when at home they are free in the house or garden and each must also have a weekly run. Near my home was a lovely park where there was a lake and here we would often go. I soon discovered I had not just a dog who was fond of water but an aquaholic. I had only to go within a quarter of a mile of water and Mandy smelt it and soon was in it. So she often went into the lake in Acton Park and when we went to the seaside she was soon in the sea, too. If we were on one of our country walks and there was a pond, or even a ditch, Mandy was soon in it. Sadly, this trait in her was to lead to her downfall.

Mandy was a very good dog while she was at the hospital. But she was also a Labrador who always needed something in her mouth. She had toys she played with in the house and garden and always carried around with her, but when we were out, if there was not something for her to grab legitimately, she would grab it illegitimately. Along the road from our house was a family whose son, David, had a twenty-first birthday party to which I was invited. The young man himself came along to escort me to the party. I knew it would be somewhat crowded so I left Mandy at home and went and joined in the refreshments with the other guests. "Oh, do go and fetch Mandy," said my hostess. So David and I collected Mandy on her lead. Once in the house, where the party was now in full swing, I took off her collar. She flew into the lounge and before you could say "Knife" with a "Woof", she had downed a piece of twenty-first birthday cake from the bottom of the trolley. It wasn't really that was stealing. Rather that Miss Mandy had to have something in her mouth. I, of course, was not at all pleased but the assembled company thought it was fabulous!

At one stage I went to London to stay with my aunt, Annie May Taylor, who was my father's sister. She always had a purse full of change on a table near the front door so if tradesmen came she had her money at the ready. One day, as she went out, before I could get Mandy and put on her collar, she leaped up to the table top, stole the purse and scattered its contents all over the floor. I had a fine time locating the money and putting it back in its proper place.

The day before we were due to leave Mandy had been taken on to Clapham Common for her run. We brought her back to the house, took off her collar and lead whereupon she flew into the breakfast room and made a bee line for the bottom of the trolley on which was a sponge sandwich specially made by my aunt for our tea. Mandy grabbed it and was soon running around with it in her mouth. She did manage to eat some sponge, too, before we took the bulk away from her, but it was inedible by us. Partly of course we took the sponge away from her because she had to learn, if that was possible, that she could not have what she took.

Mandy was always a good traveller by car, bus or train. But unfortunately one Sunday some friends from the Wirral came over with one of my godsons who was about fourteen. We had been out in the car for lunch and were going along a rather narrow country lane to some woods where Mandy was to have a run. Round a corner came a young man in a sports car, travelling far too fast. My friend John pulled his car into the side and came to a halt but the young man was unable to stop and banged into us. I held Mandy as his sports car made its impact on ours so that though she had a bump on the dashboard she did not really get hurt. Sadly, however, from that day onwards Mandy was always nervous about travelling by car. To start with she was quite happy but once she had been in the vehicle for five or ten minutes she began to pant and be disturbed. This grieved me greatly and I hoped she would get over it but she never did.

Unfortunately her nervousness spread to buses and trains which was awkward for me, the more so as I found it difficult to see her so upset. On one of my travels with Mandy I nearly lost her altogether. We were staying with friends in Angelsey who had also had a Labrador dog, called Gyp. Mandy and Gyp were great friends and they would run around a big garden wildly, enjoying each other's company. But Mandy was apt to squeeze under a gate and disappear. Once or twice she did this but fortunately in the end I got her safely back.

In early 1972 I was asked by the County Commissioner for the Girl Guide's Association if I would become a District Commissioner. I had been a Girl Guide in my youth but had lost contact after I lost my sight and knew nothing about its adult hierarchy. I certainly did not feel equipped to run a Company. But when asked to become a District Commissioner I felt it was something I would like to do but replied that I was only prepared to take it on if I could be convinced I could do the job adequately.

My great friend, Hilda Nield, whom I had met in hospital in 1948, had a sister who had been in guiding all her life. I said I would think about the proposal and consult my friend's sister. Her advice was simple: get yourself a good secretary and you will be perfectly all right. So I became a District Commissioner, though I did have a great deal to learn. My secretary, Merle, was marvellous and taught me much. I realised as I got into the swing of the job it was a task which was going to bring me much pleasure.

I had always regarded the Girl Guide movement highly. It was excellent for both younger and older girls but before I could handle them I thought I must receive training. I found out that the Welsh guide house in mid-Wales was hosting a Commissioner's Training course. So I approached the guider in charge and asked if I could attend together with Mandy? They would be delighted to have us both they replied saying that as I would have my dog accompanying me I would be allocated a single room. Unfortunately a fortnight later I heard there was an insufficient number of bookings so the course was cancelled. I then heard of another training course for the whole of Wales, applied and once again Mandy and I were accepted. We went by car and as I walked into the hotel in Llanwrtyd Wells, where the course was taking place, Mandy and I were met by the Secretary of the Welsh Girl Guide Movement, who made us both feel very welcome.

She took us up in the lift and along to my bedroom. It was quite a tortuous way as we had to go through three fire doors. I put my luggage down in my bedroom and was accompanied back to the lift. "Do you think you will be all right now?" the Guide secretary asked. I felt I could manage so Mandy and I found our way back to the bedroom once the secretary had gone downstairs. I was delighted when we reached it safely for Mandy stopped first time at the right door, which was extremely good since we had only gone there once in both directions. Her skill was all the more surprising since there were several corners to negotiate as well as the three fire doors. Now I was able to unpack. Then Mandy and I found the lift, went downstairs and walked into the hall where we knew no-one. Without Mandy I could not have coped. But with her beside me I had great confidence.

On arrival I was given a name tag to wear which made it easy for people to introduce themselves to me. I had a wonderful weekend. Mandy did, too, with free runs in the grounds. The training we were given was excellent partly because I could learn from the experienced guiders present in the workshops, and when on Sunday evening I packed up my uniform and was collected by friends I felt much more able to cope with my duties as a Guide Commissioner. We had dinner together and then my Anglesey friends, Randolph and Gwynna, who were in the area for the end of the fishing season, came and collected Mandy and me and took us to the lovely country pub where we were to stay. We had a good night; then next morning went for a walk in the woods with their pet labrador, Gyp. Once again Mandy and Gyp had a splendid time together. Then after lunch we decided to go on a country nature trail along the upper reaches of the River Towey. My friend's husband backed his car right by the gate from where we were to start the trail so the dogs would be safe. They went through immediately, free running, with us following.

It wasn't an easy path but Randolph went ahead and kept his eye on the two dogs. Gwynna and I followed. Twice I heard him say "Mandy, no." "What's she doing, Randolph?" I enquired. "She's got her eye on the river," he replied. "Oh, do be careful with Mandy," I said, "because she is an awful aquaholic." We went on quite happily for a while; then the path became very difficult where it had worn away. Here there was a fallen tree so you had to climb down a slope and duck under the tree. I picked my way carefully, with Randolph helping me. The next thing I heard him saying was "Mandy, Mandy." I knew what had happened immediately. Mandy was off into the river. I yelled and I whistled but the bank was so steep once Mandy had started to run down it even if she wished to obey me and come back she would not be able to stop. "Has she gone in the river?" Randolph asked. I replied quite confidently "Oh, she'll come out in a minute, once she's had a splash in the water." "I'll go down and get her," he responded, leaving me and Gwynna on the path.

He went down the path to the river and I was still happy about the situation. Then I heard Gwynna say "Oh no, oh no, Randolph's waded into the river." She sat on the river bank and hid her head in her hands. I stood there, frozen and waited and waited and waited. After about half an hour, soaked up to his armpits, Randolph returned. He had been unable to find Mandy.

"I saw her run down and into a pool," he reported, "and then some trees obscured my view and I could not see what happened." He had gone down and found two rocks very close to one another. It was, he told us, a wild part of the river, with water rushing at a tremendous pace between the rocks. Mandy must have been swished through this gap into another pool in the middle of which was a big rock. He could only assume Mandy had been sucked into this pool, he said, "bumped her head on the rock and been knocked out somewhere below water level."

"What are we going to do?" I asked. "I'll go down and search again," Randolph volunteered. He searched and searched, but there was no sign of Mandy. "I wonder if she got to the other side," he suggested. So, taking his own dog with him, he went to the far side of the river and made another thorough search. But there was still no trace of Mandy. Lower down there were two fishermen and we went and spoke to them. "Have you seen a Labrador dog?" we asked, describing Mandy in some detail. They had not; but they, too, came and helped in the search.

On our way back to our accommodation we called at some stables nearby to tell them what had happened and ask them to look out in case there was any news of Mandy, which they promised to do. When we reached the pub, very late for dinner, the other guests were devastated when we told them what had occurred. I had no dinner that night; nor did I have much sleep either.

Next morning guests who were staying for the fishing said they would go to the accident spot and continue the search. The men said they thought Mandy might be caught up in the second pool, where Randolph had suggested Mandy had probably banged her head. They spent two hours clearing the tree trunks and debris which had become congested at its outlet to free the water; but of Mandy there was no sign at all.

We rang up the police and told them of the accident. They promised to do all they could to publicise the disappearance of Mandy in case she had got out of the river, frightened, and had then run away. Next day we discovered the news had got into the Western Mail. I knew then I must do something about the Guide Dog Association so I rang up the Bolton centre and told Derek Carver, the controller, there had been a terrible accident. "Are you all right, Miss Dudley?" he asked. "Yes, I'm all right," I said, "it's Mandy." He asked what the trouble was and I explained. "Oh, Mr Carver," I went on, "we were taking care of her. My friends are most caring. They had a pet dog with them. I feel so terrible about what has happened." "Miss Dudley," he countered, "you must not feel like that. Guide dogs after all are dogs which are trained to do a very special job of work. It is a demanding job and it builds up nervous tension in them. If they didn't have freedom to run and be dogs they would never be able to do their work. Please, please, don't feel guilty in any way. Mandy has not had an accident when she was in harness so please don't worry."

I came back to Wrexham at the end of the week and found everyone there knew what had occurred. They, too, were upset, because both Mandy and I were very well known in the town. I became very concerned when I had been back some ten days because I heard that a local infant and junior school were raising money to buy me a new dog and knew the Guide Dog Association had a policy that all money raised for its work went into the main fund with dogs provided for each blind or partially sighted student from this fund alone. "What's my line, Mr Carver?" I asked when I rang him up. "Well, you know the policy as well as I do," he replied. "Indeed I do," I answered," and have always stressed it when giving talks about the Association." "You cannot stop these children saying they are raising money to buy you a new dog," he continued. "We must not think about it too much. Don't worry about it." Before I went back to Bolton for my new dog the children had raised £1,250. I was overwhelmed but then the children at the schools had known Mandy as I had been there with her.

The weekend after the fatal accident friends of mine from Wrexham went down the Towey valley and asked if the stables had any further information. They told them and then my friends re-visited the site of the accident itself but the situation was hopeless. They reported to me that the people at the stables had been very upset on the night I went and told them what had happened to Mandy and that the owner of the stables had said "I couldn't tell her, she was too upset. But I knew she would never see that dog again." It appeared that even huntsmen had been in the river after their dogs who had tried to swim in the currents, but they, too, "had just disappeared."

I suppose it's a legend that has sprung up because of the wild nature of the valley but near the spot where Mandy went into the river there is a cave up in the hills which overlooks the river. It's called Twm Sion-Catti (catti meaning cave.) Twm Sion was a bandit at the time of one of the civil wars between England and Wales and troops were sent to catch him because he caused such havoc to the English. But they had never caught him because he had this vantage point and was able to see the English troops advancing. Apparently he had just disappeared into the Welsh hills which he knew like the back of his hand. So a legend had sprung up that anything beautiful which passed the cave disappeared for Twm Sion had wafted it away.

Perhaps, I thought, the legend had sprung up because animals were lost in the raging torrent in the Towey where my darling Mandy had disappeared for ever.

Chapter 6

Vida

Mandy had disappeared in September 1972. By November I had a phone call from the Bolton training centre to say they had a suitable replacement for me. So again I packed my bags, obtained leave of absence from the hospital and went to Lancashire to meet my new friend. I arrived on a Saturday and immediately got to know my fellow students. By Sunday I was in the grounds with my trainer to re-learn footwork, voice control and hand signals, with my trainer pretending to be the dog.

On Monday afternoon I was in my room after lunch when my trainer, Phil Stott, knocked on my door, came in and said "This is

Vida." It was the Queen's Silver Wedding day and is a day I will always remember. Vida was gorgeous with a lovely head, which was pure Labrador. "When you leave Vida in your room, Miss Dudley," Phil Stott told me, "you will have to put a bucket on her head." I looked at him askance. "Why on earth must I do that?" I queried. "Well, after she finished her training on Friday, the vet removed a little growth between two toes on her front foot and put a couple of stitches in. As you'll see, she's got a bandage on," Phil explained. "While she is with you she can be watched," he went on, "but when you come for meals, as the new dogs don't come with their owners, you will need to put this bucket on her head to prevent her chewing off the bandage." He then produced a small plastic bucket, which had its bottom cut out. To this a dog collar had been attached, with holes cut through the plastic, some pieces of bandage binding the collar to enable the bucket itself to be popped over the dog's head and fastened to the collar. Thus a dog could walk around perfectly well, see where it was going and even lie down on its bed with no difficulty. But it could not get its mouth down to its foot.

I was now left with Vida for two hours who was relaxed though a little unsettled because she could still hear Phil Stott coming up and down the corridor as he took other dogs to their owners. However I was more popular with Vida when it came to feeding time. The food was in fact produced in the kennels but then put into numbered lockers for each student to feed his or her own dog each evening.

Once we settled down together Vida and I began our training. From the word go she turned out to be an absolute dream. She walked beautifully and concentrated on her work. I was in a seventh heaven. During the years I was with Mandy the trainers had brought into existence an obstacle course which was in a driveway in their grounds. There were obstacles to the right and left and things overhead, too. You started with your dog at one end and weaved your way, both left and right, to the other. When you got there you put down the handle which guided your dog, gave much praise and then turned round and came back.

It was good training for it taught a student actively to follow his or her dog. When you go round to the left, for example, you have to hold your dog back a little and increase your step. When you go to the right, you hold back a little and give your dog time to come round to you to level up again. On the way back there is a trap which the dog walks into. You say "Hup, hup, come on, good girl," and when a dog goes straight on nothing happens. If this goes wrong you have to take half a step back, tickle your dog's head and say "Good girl." As soon as you step back a little and the dog has room, it turns round in front of you, turns back, then left round a corner and goes to the end. Now is the time for yet more praise after you have put down your dog's handle.

Vida was marvellous at this obstacle course from the word go. I must have had a grin from ear to ear as Phil Stott said to me "Miss Dudley, that was super. But don't tell the others how well you did because everybody is trying to do their best and each student has a different ability. All dogs are different, too, and some have not had dogs before. Moreover, we all have good and bad days. It never does, you see, to say "I've had a marvellous day," because you might be talking to someone who has had a rotten one and vice versa."

Once during training Vida was going down Devonshire Road near the centre. But unknown to me obstacles had been put in the way. Try as I would she would not find the kerb. "Why won't she find the curb?" I kept asking, telling myself at the same time to remain cool. When she did she would merely sit. Eventually we did reach the centre and find the grooming room. "You were a bit puzzled in Devonshire Road when Vida would not get off the kerb," my trainer remarked when we had the customary chat after the training exercise. "But you did the right thing. You trusted her, which is what you have always to do." "Why would she only go so far and then sit?" I enquired. "Well," the trainer explained, "I put a wooden strip right down the road." A few months later, when I met a similar situation in real life, I had reason to be grateful to him.

As the days went on Vida and I became more and more attached to one another. She became less interested in Phil Stott, too. "You'll find that once you get home," he observed, "you'll bond very quickly because the only person Vida will know is you." He also advised me to arrange for a meeting between my brother's pet dog, Trudi, a guide dog reject from the Leamington Spa centre, and Vida, on neutral ground when he and his wife came from Warwickshire, where they now lived, to see me. This we arranged so my brother's fears that he ought not to have brought Trudi with him were allayed the more so as from the start both Vida and Trudi got on splendidly.

Two days later, on December 12th, I came home and settled down. Phil came to see me on the 14th and we walked to the hospital from my home. Once there we taught Vida how to find the staff room and the physiotherapy department. Before we set out I told Mr Stott my brother and his wife would like us to spend Christmas with them but that I thought it was a bit early to do this as we had hardly been home long enough. "I'll tell you what I think when we get back from the hospital," Phil had replied. "No problems at all," he stated when we arrived home. "Vida was super this morning. But you must take her out working each day."

So Vida and I set off for Warwickshire for Christmas after she had been with me at home only for ten days. We went into a nearby small town each day to do some work. In all we stayed five days with my family, then returned home and started back at the hospital on the first Monday of the new year. Vida again found the staff room beautifully and the physiotherapy department, too. I showed Vida her bed, but didn't fasten her because I felt she would be perfectly all right without.

She stayed there for about half an hour but then joined me as I worked with two men who were playing with a medicine ball, mistaking an instruction I had given them. "Sorry, darling, not you," I said. "You go back and sit on your bed." Vida complied and never left it the whole time she was at the hospital except when going with me at coffee-time and for lunch. She was lovely when we lunched in the hospital's dining-room, normally three times each week, which we did from 1972 to 1979. She knew exactly where I sat and would wind her way round the tables to find my seat.

Sometimes I lunched with Margaret Millar, a friend I made at the hospital, who was Principal of the North Wales School of Radiography and on occasions when we left the dining-room Vida would take a very circuitous route out. "Vida went a long way round today, didn't she?" Margaret would comment. "Yes, why?" I responded. "Well," Margaret replied, "there was a chip on the floor which she looked at. But she seemed to say to herself, "I mustn't touch that chip so I won't go near it in case it jumps out at me and I get blamed.""

Vida was fantastic, especially on walks. It was nothing for us on a Sunday morning to go out for a two hour walk to the far side of Wrexham, across traffic lights, roundabouts and the like. She was certainly the most brilliant dog I ever had. After she had been with me a year it was decided to build a new police station in Wrexham. The principal road from my home, once I had walked down the side roads, was along a grass verge and a tree lined park avenue which led you right to the centre of town. It was decided to build the police station at the bottom end of Park Avenue, which was therefore radically altered once bulldozers and builders moved in.

Yet it was still possible to walk up and down the avenue and I used to do this with Vida. We would start one way coming back and get as far as we could before I would say "Hup, hup, good girl." Vida would then take half a step back, then round in front of me she would come just as she had come out of the trap she had negotiated in training. Then she would wend her way back, seeking to find another way, maybe start on her new route. But finding she could not do this any more she would turn back a second time. Each time she led me safely through the alterations and though they were never the same she brought me safely home.

Vida in fact saw a problem and solved it in her mind very quickly indeed. Working with Vida was like walking on air. In fact I began to forget I couldn't see, even forget Vida was doing all the guiding for we walked along in such perfect harmony I felt I was the guide. But I wasn't: it was my lovely Vida who was the real guide.

In spring 1979 my radiography friend Margaret, another great friend Doris Browne and I, went on a self-catering holiday in a cottage in the Cotswolds near Broadway. It was in an area known as Middle Hill, with woods nearby. The situation was idyllic and we were able to do an enormous amount of walking with Vida running free. She had a splendid time. Until then she had not really come across many stiles but she soon learned to jump them. So successful was the holiday that we went again that autumn and once more in the spring of 1980.

We enjoyed a lovely holiday then, with cooked breakfasts, packed lunches after walking all morning, as the sandwiches and drinks from flasks we had brought sustained us. Vida had a special drink though she seldom needed it as streams and brooks provided her with sustenance. On our last day we were coming back down Middle Hill and talking away when Margaret said suddenly "My goodness, Vida leaped out of there pretty quickly." "Leaped out of where?" I asked. "Oh, a pile of dead leaves," Margaret replied. "She shot out of there as if she'd been shot with a gun." "Probably she pricked herself on a bramble," I countered.

When we reached our holiday cottage I fed Vida who then got on her bed for a good sleep while we had a meal. Early on Saturday morning I popped her harness on and took her out into the nearby woods and stood there while she had a run. Then I put her harness on again and took her back indoors. As her feet were now wet I said "Come here, let mum wipe your feet, there's a good girl." As I wiped her front right paw she said "Oww!" "Oh dear," I sympathised, "you have got a poorly paw."

We now put Vida on the floor of the kitchen and Margaret and Doris examined her foot. They couldn't see anything, no thorn or cut, so we packed up and started for home. Now I am a great believer in Epsom Salts soaks for any infection. So I brought a tin and when we reached my house I found my enamel jug and made up a potion which was strong. I let it cool first, then put Vida's foot in the Epsom Salts, leaving it to soak. Then I wiped it and looked to see if she was all right, which she seemed to be.

I didn't take her for a Sunday walk, telling myself I would give her foot several soaks and hope that by the evening Vida would be well. Margaret and I went to Doris for supper that evening but as Vida walked I could tell she was not enjoying putting her weight on her foot. I therefore gave her yet another soak when we returned home deciding I would take her to the vet's after my work at the hospital if by next evening she was still unwell.

Vida ate her supper that evening and went to bed calmly but next morning when she went down the stairs she nearly fell. Again she was having trouble putting any weight on the affected foot. "What's the matter, sweetheart?" I said soothingly once we were in the hall. "Is that foot sore?" I now took hold of her right leg and nearly had a fit for I found that the entire leg was swollen and hard. "No wonder she nearly fell down the stairs," I said to myself. I still took her out, however, put her in her run and brought her in and gave her breakfast. Then I rang Margaret and asked her if she could take Vida to the vet there and then. I told the hospital, too, about my problems and said I would be late arriving for work.

"Oh I think Vida must have sprained her leg on holiday," the vet said. "I'm not very sure about that," I replied, for the swelling had not occurred until Monday morning whereas I had known something had been wrong the previous Saturday. "There's nothing broken and I can see nothing in her leg, so I think it is a sprain," he countered. "I'll give you some Denvet to paint on it," a substance I knew was used for racing greyhounds and for whippets. Once home I put some on Vida's foot, the second dose she had received for the vet had already rubbed some Denvet on her leg. That afternoon I left for the hospital leaving Vida on her bed in the lounge. When I came downstairs for supper that night clearly she was very poorly indeed. She didn't want her supper very much. I continued to apply the Denvet but by Tuesday morning she was no better so back to the vet I went. He agreed to X-ray her which showed conclusively that nothing had been broken.

Margaret had read out to me from the instructions for the use of Denvet that it was more efficacious if the fur of an animal was shaved off. I told the vet this fact who replied suggesting I did not want this done. "I don't mind," I told him. "I want Vida better." On the Monday he had suggested my guide dog needed above all a rest but that would be difficult for me. "It's not difficult at all," I had replied. "If she's to have rest, rest she must have." "Well," he now said, "I won't shave her leg. I'll clip her fur." He began down by her claws, then exclaimed "Oh! Oh!" "What have you found?" I asked. "This dog has been bitten," he told me. "Bitten?" I queried. "Yes, I think she's been bitten by an adder," he explained. "I'm sure she has," I now agreed because I remembered one of my friends had read out to me the contents of a notice at the top of the woods which had warned people to beware of adders. "What do we have to do to beware of adders?" I had asked at the time and they had said they did not know. "I guarantee," Margaret said now, "that when Vida jumped out of that pile of leaves she'd disturbed an adder which had been hibernating in them."

The previous winter had been bitterly cold right into spring and there had been, I now recalled, several pieces in the newspapers about adders being disturbed before they were properly awake, either by animals or people. If so disturbed out would come their fangs and they would bite. Clearly this was what had happened to Vida, with the adder's poison eventually reaching her whole leg. Mercifully, because I had soaked it in hot water with Epsom Salts, I had saved Vida's life the vet suggested.

Now I continued to soak Vida's leg with Denvet, though I suspect it had little effect. Gradually, however, the swelling subsided and in three or four days Vida was back to her normal self. We had undergone a terrible fright which had made me especially concerned as in the first instance her malady had been incorrectly diagnosed. I now felt if her fur had been clipped when I had first seen the vet the adder's fang marks would have been found. Eventually of course the fur grew again but to the end of Vida's life you could still see a little red patch with two marks where she had been bitten.

The winter of 1976/77 was very severe in Wrexham. A heavy fall of snow had been followed by three or four days and nights of frost, then more snow, then weeks of frost. The roads and pavements were icy, too. The snow plough had been along the roads to clear them but had piled the snow into the gutters. The footpaths themselves were like skating rinks. Pedestrians in fact stopped using them, the few who were willing to risk the bad weather conditions walking along the edges of the roads, which was not very safe because they were now narrower because of the snow in the gutters.

Despite the bad weather, which lasted for three months, I still had to get to the hospital and back so Vida and I struggled day after day on the route. It was very hard going because guide dogs are taught to walk on footpaths, to cross roads straight and be on the roads as little time as possible. Consequently Vida was not prepared to walk along the side of the roads, for she considered this to be unsafe. Our proper place she knew was on the footpaths. Each time we came to a road crossing, however, we had to climb over a pile of snow, get down on to the road itself, then cross it and clamber over another pile of snow at the far side before we could continue.

The footpaths continued to be slippery. I had to wear a pair of chains on the bottom of my boots, cross chains on their soles and a chain across the heel, which certainly helped. I had a stick with me as well but it took Vida and I twice as long to reach the hospital and get home again after work than normally. By the time I got there I was completely exhausted. I used to leave extra early so I could have ten minutes to sit down and have a coffee before starting work. The struggle went on for weeks but Vida never once let me down. She seemed to realise things were difficult for me so she walked much more slowly and was very careful when we were climbing over the piles of snow.

Those few weeks, together with the sudden death of a close friend, left their toll and I succumbed to a bad bout of influenza. During my years at the hospital I had taken very little time off but now I was away for six weeks. I was in bed for ten days unable either to eat or drink much at all. The only fluid I could take was Lucozade. One day the doctor came and a friend took Vida out on a lead for her walk and to give her free runs three times a week. For the rest of the time she had to stay with me though she was able to go out into the garden.

After four weeks the doctor came to find out how I was. "I'm ashamed to say I don't feel much better," I told him. "Don't feel ashamed" he replied, "You should never have been struggling to the hospital as you did all those weeks." "I had to go," I expostulated, "I was their employee and there were patients needing treatment." "Well," he replied firmly, "You are not going back until you are really fit." Hilda now rang from Cheshire to invite me to stay for a few days to see if a change of air would help my recovery. She also invited Vida saying she and Mary would look after us. For the first three days I felt really down in the dumps but now most times I was able to eat. We went for little walks on the hill where Vida had a free run and one morning when I woke up I felt so much better. From then on I picked up and didn't look back.

I was staying with Hilda during the celebration of the Queen's Silver Jubilee, marking her twenty-five years on the throne. When Hilda brought me home again in the post was a note from the postman to say they had tried to deliver a parcel and had failed. So when Vida and I went into town a couple of days later to do the shopping we made our way to the sorting office. We had never been there before but I knew where to turn and said to Vida "Hup, hup, hup, find the door, find the door," which she did. We went in and the postman brought me a package. "There you are, Miss Dudly," he said in a knowing way, indicating there was no charge when I asked what I had to pay.

Thanking him Vida and I went home and called in on the way to have a coffee with my friend Doris. I told her I'd been to collect a parcel and would open it in a minute. I took it out and left it on the table meanwhile until Doris said "Excuse me, I'm being very nosey, but will you open the parcel because it's something special." "Is it?" I countered. "Yes," she replied, "It's from Buckingham Palace." "From Buckingham Palace?" I exclaimed, looking at her. "Never." "It is," she said. I opened the parcel and found a beautiful case inside, with a Queen's

Silver Jubilee medal inside. I was speechless. Then I realised why the postman had spoken in a rather special way.

One afternoon in the spring of 1979 I had a phone call from Sir Watkin Williams Wynn, the Lord Lieutenant of Denbighshire, whom I had met on several occasions and whose wife had been a patient of mine. "Miss Dudley," he said, "I wondered if you would like an invitation to one of the Royal Garden Parties?" I was delighted and said so, whereupon he said my dog could accompany me and that I could also take a friend with me. I was over the moon and wondered who to ask. Clearly it needed to be someone who herself had given public service. I thought soon of Hilda Nield, my friend in Cheshire and of her Red Cross work in southern Africa, who was delighted to come with me when I suggested the idea to her. In due course therefore both Hilda and I received the formal invitation to Buckingham Palace.

I bought myself a new cream and navy suit and a navy hat and tried to make myself as presentable as possible. Early on the morning of the Garden Party itself we set off for London by train from Crewe. Once in London we took Vida into Regent's Park for her run, then had lunch at the VAD Club, now the New Cavendish. That over, we ordered a taxi to take us to Buckingham Palace, put the appropriate sticker on its windscreen and set off. We stopped en route by Hyde Park to give Vida another run, then joined the queue of taxis in the Mall waiting for Buckingham Palace gates to be opened at 2 o'clock.

It was a beautiful, sunny day, though there was a tiny breeze. We got out of our taxi in the Palace itself and followed the people in front of us through some of the downstairs rooms and so out on to the terrace, then down some steps on to the lawn.

Hilda gave me a description of the gardens and the lake and the beautiful flowers and explained to me that on one side blue and white marquees had been set up for the guests where in due course tea would be served.

Before the royal party itself came out guests were ushered into groups forming pathways through which the Royal Family would walk. Hilda, Vida and I were at the front of the pathway down which the Duke of Edinburgh was to come. Shortly before the royal party came on to the terrace several people were presented to the Duke of Edinburgh and I, with Vida, found I was to be one of them.

The royal party then came on to the lawn, the Queen going down one pathway, the Duke of Edinburgh another, with the Prince of Wales and Princess Anne (as she was then) also there. When the Duke of Edinburgh came to me one of the gentlemen at arms introduced me and the Duke of Edinburgh shook hands with me, asked where I came from, what work I did and then spoke about Vida. He thought her a beautiful looking dog and told me he very much admired the work of guide dogs. Shaking hands with me again, he then passed on.

When the royal party reached the tea room they went inside and we guests went to the other marquees, where there were tables and chairs set outside. We sat down, Vida sitting proudly by my side, while we had our thin cucumber sandwiches and dainty cakes off beautiful china with the royal crest on it. After tea the royal family made its way back into Buckingham Palace, turned and waved, after which guests were allowed to mingle and walk around the grounds. Hilda and I thought we would walk round the lake and had got a third of the way round when I turned and said to Hilda "Do you think it would be all right if we let Vida loose for a little run?" Hilda thought it was, so I took off Vida's collar, lead and harness, and she ran round, going down into the thick grass by the edge of the lake, where she poked around. Everybody was looking at her and admiring her. When she had her spell of freedom I put on her harness again, we walked back along the lawns, up the palace steps and onto the terrace and then out into the Buckingham Palace forecourt. Once outside we hailed a taxi to take us to the station and then caught our train home. It had been a wonderful occasion and I had been so proud of Vida, who had looked so smart with a new harness and a special grooming.

In March 1980 I had to retire from the hospital. I had often heard people say, "Oh, I can't wait to retire," and that they were looking forward to their retirement but that was not my attitude at all. I still loved my work at the hospital and its life so I was very sad to be finishing. The last morning there it was very touching. As it happened all the patients were men and they brought me cards wishing me a happy retirement. Two also brought flowers. I was often on the verge of tears. When lunchtime came there was a party and a presentation. I left the physiotherapy department itself and went the long way round to the recreation hall through out-patients and walked across it as it thronged with both patients and staff. Vida proudly led me in my uniform for the last time and after I'd gone up the main corridor with Vida I arrived at the place where the party was to be held.

One or two people said nice things about me and my work and I had to reply, lump or no lump in my throat. I spoke about my happy years at both the hospitals in which I had worked and made them laugh when I said when I started I had worn a long white starched coat and "a sort of nun's veil" on my head. "Today," I added, "you can see I'm here in navy trousers and a white jacket. So we've come a long way in those years." After I had said farewell to my colleagues, Vida and I came downstairs. I thought I would take the long way back to the staff room so down the long corridor we went, though out-patients again, walking very straight, my chin held high.

I thought never again will Vida and I walk through the hospital with me in uniform. Going into the staff room I changed. As there was nobody there I said "Goodbye staff room, you've been a wonderful place for both Vida and me." Then we left the hospital. I hardly remember the journey home as I had a lump in my throat and tears in my eyes. I merely said to Vida "We're going home," and she brought me safely there with scarcely a word, or even recognition, from me.

Chapter 7

More of Vida

Fortunately that night I had a Guide function - I had in fact become more involved in the movement from 1975 when I had been appointed a Divisional Commissioner - so I had to pull myself together and tell my mind that I must shape a new life. This I now began to do. Moreover I still had the companionship of Vida. In May 1980, some two months after my retirement, I had been out with Vida and called for coffee at Doris' house. I popped my mail on her table and asked her to read it to me. She was keen to open the mail immediately. "I'd like to have the letter that's on top," she said firmly. "It's from the Prime Minister's office." I replied flippantly saying "Oh, I'm quite sure the Prime Minister's asking me to join the cabinet," and laughed. Opening the letter I handed it to Doris. She told me it asked if I were offered an MBE (for my hospital work I imagined) would I be prepared to accept it. Once again I was speechless. I could not believe my great fortune.

I wrote back and said I would be delighted to accept an MBE and would be pleased to attend the investiture at Buckingham Palace. I explained, too, that as I was a guide dog owner if it were possible I would like to bring my dog with me. I waited for the reply with bated breath which when it came said my dog would also be welcome in Buckingham Palace and would be suitably looked after during the investiture itself.

The letter had told me I could bring two guests with me. Who was I to invite? I would have liked to invite my brother and his wife but by this time they were living in Sussex, though they did visit me twice a year to help with odd jobs like gardening and sewing. The people who really helped me were my friend Hilda in Cheshire and Margaret, the radiographer. But my two oldest friends were Hilda and Doris, with Margaret being my newest friend, so I settled for them.

The first Saturday in June, which is the Queen's official birthday, I knew the announcement would be in the paper. By then I had not been told definitely I would be granted an MBE, merely asked if one were offered would I accept it? I thought because the letter about the medal was only known to Doris and myself it was a secret but I became very suspicious on the Friday night when about 11 p.m. my phone went and I found myself talking to a reporter from a South Wales newspaper, who was checking that I had been a physiotherapist for a number of years and confirming the names of the hospitals in which I had worked.

When Saturday morning arrived Doris was at the newsagents as soon as it opened. She ran home with the paper, looked at the honours list and phoned me to say my name was on it. When the news finally came out there was much excitement, with friends arriving for a glass of sherry to celebrate with me. By October, when the investiture was to be held, Doris and I had been to the shops to buy a new outfit. Vida's harness was still in very good order from her visit to the garden party, so it now had an extra clean and polish and Vida herself a splendid grooming.

Hilda, Doris, Vida and I went to Euston and then Vida was fed in Regent's Park. After this we had dinner at the VAD Club, then went by taxi to my favourite aunt's house near Clapham Common for the night. Next morning we got up early, Vida was sent out into my aunt's garden and I gave her a quick run over with a chamois leather before the taxi came to take us to Buckingham Palace. Once there the taxi swung in through the main gate because we had to report at a different entrance from the main bulk of the visitors that day.

A footman came to open the taxi's door and we were then shown into a room where one of the Queen's staff welcomed us. He then rang for the Queen's page who was to look after me at the investiture itself. Soon he arrived in his black velvet gown and black cap. In addition a former military man, who had on all his medals, was introduced to me and told me he would look after Vida during the investiture. He would ensure she was safe and would be there to greet me at the end of the ceremony. The Queen's page asked me if I would like to go up in the lift but I said I would prefer to go up the main staircase as I was sure my guests would, too. At the top my guide told me this was where they and I parted and I was to go with him into one of the waiting rooms.

The Queen was at that time on a state visit in North Africa, so the Queen Mother was taking the investiture. My guide, who looked after me so splendidly, taught me exactly what to do and when my turn came to be presented he swept me into the ballroom as if I were a duchess. I was then presented with my MBE, the Queen Mother had a few words with me and I was swept out again to sit on a red damask chair. The investiture over, I went down the main staircase again to the reception room where the retainer was waiting for me with Vida, who told me she had been very good, even having a walk in the Palace grounds. "She has also been down to the Queen's kitchen and has had two biscuits," I was told. "She's been a very lucky little girl," I answered. "She's beautiful, madam," came the reply.

Hilda had arranged a lunch party for me at the VAD club, to which my brother and his wife came, as well as Doris' daughter and of course Vida. Then my brother drove us back to Euston and we went home to Wrexham. Vida, I suppose, was tired by the end of that day but she hadn't put a foot wrong. I told her she was "a real royal guide dog."

I was still missing hospital life but I kept busy, going for walks with Vida, visiting friends and doing the shopping. My job as Divisional Commissioner for Wrexham Guides involved me in attending County executive meetings and other functions so that took up much time, too. I also had divisional meetings, which I held in my house. As I also Chaired the local branch of the Guide Dogs for the Blind Association I did considerable speaking on its behalf as well. Some of this required preparation beforehand but often, as I knew my subject like the back of my hand and was by now well used to public speaking, I was able to speak off the cuff.

Vida continued to be superb at leading me, whether over pedestrian crossings, through traffic lights or crossing the market square. Once I decided to visit friends who had recently moved, a forty minute walk away. It was Christmas-time and I only vaguely knew how to get to their new house. A school teacher patient filled me in on the details, which were very complicated, and off Vida and I went. We had to negotiate pavements, turn right and then right again; find iron railings at the end of one road (put there to stop cyclists crossing); then cross left and go right and after that walk straight over a wide open space. I took a deep breath and urged Vida on. She found the railings all right; but then sat down after only three steps across the grass because she expected to have her harness removed so she could have her customary free run. Shortly after this episode she even found a phone box in the middle of a path which we had to locate.

In late April 1981 Doris, Margaret and myself, went for a holiday in the west Cotswolds at Driftcombe, near Bisley, the scene of Laurie Lee's novel about adolescence, *Cider with Rosie*. Once there I gave Vida a scamper around the cottage and we all helped to prepare the evening meal on the electric cooker. Doris cooked the meal itself, while Margaret and I took Vida for a good run. It was the first of several beautiful country walks staying in a holiday cottage which was both quiet and isolated, with a nearby brook, woods and rising ground, on which Vida especially enjoyed herself.

Just as we arrived back from our walk it began to rain which continued heavily all evening. We went to sleep, Vida on her travelling bed, and slept well. Next morning it was my task to light the fire. Doris had beaten me down, however, and now greeted me with the news that there was no electricity and that there had been a tremendous fall of snow during the night. I called Margaret, who was much younger than both of us, and she came downstairs immediately. Clearly the fire must be lit quickly, especially as Doris was then in her mid-70's. When this was burning well we all dressed in our warmest clothes, took blankets from our beds and had a cold breakfast. But what could we do with Vida? She had been given her breakfast, but when we opened the cottage door and said "Out you go, there's a good girl," she went a few steps and no further. Clearly, Margaret told us, she would not be able to function as the snow was reaching halfway up her body. Accordingly we found a shovel and brush, cleared away some of the snow and made a path which Vida could trot along, then cleared a space in the snow and banged it down so she could have that as her toilet.

Once Vida was back inside the cottage we filled the kettle and in girl guide fashion put a match in it so the water did not get smokey and had coffee. Soon we had a visitor, a rather arty young man, who was clearly a poet. He had known there were visitors at the cottage and had walked from his with some raw meat and vegetables for us to use. He sat with us for a while, then went on his way. We were pleased, for we thought we could cook his gifts. We could also cut up a shoulder of lamb we had brought and put it in a saucepan with vegetables, so making stew by cooking it on the fire. We were having another coffee to help us keep warm when we had two more visitors, a husband and wife this time, who also knew there were three ladies staying at the cottage. They told us the owner, Duncan Smith, had rung them that morning and asked them to see if we were coping because our phone line was down. Seeing we were well in control they left saying they would call again next day.

We stayed in the cottage all day Sunday and Monday, but by Tuesday judged the snow was not as bad as it had been, playing havoc with the trees and breaking them. So we decided to walk up to Bisley, going through woods where Vida could run loose. She loved the snow especially. As we came to a field and approached a gate, into what should have been a lane but was still a mass of snow, a young man opened a bedroom window and shouted "Are you the three old ladies from Driftcombe with the guide dog?" We roared with laughter and admitted it! It seemed everyone was worried about us, though we ourselves were scarcely concerned at all.

When we reached Bisley we went into the pub and had a good lunch; then returned to the cottage to find snow ploughs had been along the road and that the fallen trees, which had brought down telegraph poles and cut off the electricity, were being moved. Still, however, the cottage had neither electricity nor the phone. But on the handle of the front door was a plastic bag inside of which was bread, some butter and bacon, as well as a big box of chocolates and a bottle of whisky, with a note from Duncan Smith saying he had great admiration for the three ladies and the guide dog who had fallen upon such hard times at the cottage. He hoped we would be all right.

A couple of days later the electricity returned and Margaret was able to get her car out, so we went into Stroud. My wellington boots had given way so we bought a new pair. I was very disgusted with one of Stroud's cafés. I had Vida in harness and we went into it to have coffee. But they would not allow Vida in. It was the first time I had ever been refused admission with my guide dog. In earlier days I seem to recall guide dog owners had difficulties, but by then the dogs were accepted and in places like Marks and Spencers, Woolworths and all supermarkets, where there were notices on the door which read "No dogs allowed except guide dogs and dogs for the disabled." Appalled, we left abruptly and found a café where they would accept Vida.

1981 was a special year for the Guide Dog for the Blind Association. It was its Golden Jubilee. The Association had started in Wallasey in a very small way in 1931 but by 1981 the movement had grown immensely. There were some five training centres and the movement was now well-known in Britain. To celebrate the Association decided to arrange a Thanksgiving Service in Westminster Abbey. All guide dog owners were allowed to apply for an invitation though it would not be possible for all to attend with their dogs. I therefore applied but a few days later was very disappointed to learn I had not been successful. I was speaking to the North West Regional Appeals Manager in his office in Chester and told him what had happened. "Don't worry," he told me. "There will be two invitations for the Wrexham Branch." That was fine, especially as I Chaired the branch and Margaret, who had not been with me for the Buckingham Palace events, was Treasurer. She was therefore delighted when I asked her to come with me to Westminster Abbey for the thanksgiving service.

Again Vida's harness was given an extra clean and polish. She was also made to look very smart. Once again when we arrived in London we had lunch at the VAD club and gave Vida a run in Hyde Park. As the taxi got nearer and nearer to Westminster Abbey Margaret said "Oh, there's another guide dog," then "There are two more guide dogs." The reason was simple: the Guide Dog Association had arranged for part of Hyde Park to be cordoned off for guide dog owners to take their dogs there before they went into Westminster Abbey.

The actual service was lovely. The Association, knowing guide dog owners would not be able to appreciate the visual glories of Westminster Abbey, had decided that the service would be an unforgettable event from the hearing point of view. We therefore had the Westminster Abbey choir, the senior organist and the Queen's State Trumpeters to aid the worship. One of the Abbey' staff gave a commentary and the Association's President, Princess Alexandra, arrived soon to meet the Council before processing up the aisle and the service began.

There were 2,000 people in the Abbey, including over six hundred guide dogs owners with their dogs, members from the Guide Dog Association branches, and from the training centres, as well as civic leaders and officials from the National

Association. The singing of well-known hymns like "Praise my soul the king of heaven" and "Be Thou my vision" was superb and the State Trumpeters made their sounds reverberate throughout the Abbey. There were fine prayers of thanksgiving for those who first had the vision to start the Guide Dogs Association, for those who had worked across the years to help it forward and those who did so now, for the dogs themselves and for the Association's future. Two guide dog owners read the lessons and the address was given by the then Speaker of the House of Commons, George Thomas, later Lord Tonypandy.

He was particularly delightful, with a gift of oratory rather than mere speaking. He spoke about Westminster Abbey, which reached back into Britain's past. So much history had take place there, he observed. "And today history is being made, too. For never before have some six hundred guide dogs, with their owners, been in the congregation of the Abbey." He had, apparently, had a very troubled week in the House of Commons, with MP's getting out of hand. "Your dogs are so beautifully behaved," he commented. "I wish the people with whom I have to do were half as well behaved as your wonderful dogs." There was a ripple of laughter throughout the Abbey.

At the end of the service all the dogs, who with the exception of two had been completely silent throughout, with their owners streamed out of Westminster Abbey. The bells of the Abbey rang out in the bright sunshine, the band of the Irish Guards, with their mascot, a big Irish Wolf Hound with his coat on, began to play. They then led all the people and the dogs up Birdcage Walk and eventually into the mews of Buckingham Palace, where tea was being provided. Here I met people I had not seen for many years, some from my days of training, some who were members of the Associations' Council. Princess Alexandra was there, too, who mingled with the crowds and spoke to many. This was the third time Vida had been to Buckingham Palace. Afterwards, when Margaret and I were talking about her, we no longer referred to her as Vida, but the Princess, a name we still use when we speak of her.

Wrexham Division of the Guide Association was part of the County of Clwyd, as it was then termed, and Clwyd Guides now decided to mark the Golden Jubilee of guide dogs in 1981 partly because they knew Vida, by raising enough money to pay for the training of a guide dog and its master or mistress. As a result Vida and I went to many different parts of the County, to brownie packs and guide companies, to show Vida to them. I would then talk to them about Vida and her work. They were very good to her while she was in her harness, neither speaking to her nor attempting to touch her, but when I had finished speaking and her harness was off, she would often disappear under twenty-four brownies all trying to pat her at the same time, even though she was on a long lead. When she was moulting I am afraid those brownies went home with much dog hair on their brown uniforms!

They did superbly well, raising over £1,500 to train a guide dog. As they were a youth organisation they were allowed to name a dog and so they had a competition amongst all the packs and companies and decided to call their dog Clwyd. We had to wait a little while for Clwyd to be born but eventually he was and the puppy went to Forfar Training Centre in Scotland. One of the County's Guide Companies was in Scotland, not far from Forfar, and decided they would like to visit the centre. The leading guider was talking to one of the kennel staff as other guides looked around them when suddenly a couple of them rushed up and said "We've seen a place and it says "Clwyd" over the kennel. But there isn't a dog inside." "Oh, are you interested in Clwyd?" asked the kennel girl talking with them. The guides explained they were and the reason for such interest so the Centre sent a car to find the trainer, who was out in Forfar and brought Clwyd back to meet the guides. Thus they met the dog they and their fellow members of the Clwyd Guide Association had sponsored.

By now the policy of the Association was for a yearly visit by a trainer to a guide dog and its owner. The object of this was to see them working together and make sure the dog's work was satisfactory and that the owner was doing all that should be done for the dog. Vida already had regular after-care visits but now she was ten a visit occurred every six months.

Between 1981 and 1983 life went on much as usual for Vida and me. We had walks, shopped, visited friends and went to functions. I also gave talks. In October 1982 my brother Eric and his wife came to stay with me for a week and I noticed Eric had slowed down a little. When he did some work for me in the garden it seemed to take him longer and he was not able to achieve as much in the time as on previous visits. Then in mid-December he rang me to say Iris had gone into a nursing home to have a hip replacement and that he himself was due to go into hospital in two days time. "Eric, what on earth is the matter?" I asked him. "I'm afraid one of my kidneys has packed up and I've got to have it removed," I was told. I asked some questions about what had happened and what the results of the investigations had shown and he told me that he had been advised to have a nephrectomy. "I know you'll want to come and see me in the nursing home in Eastbourne, Joyce," he conceded, "but don't come because it will be Christmas-time, the trains will be very busy and you now have an older guide dog." "Vida and I will not come and see you alone," I promised. "Now you keep your promise," he added and wishing him well I said I would. "I'm sure you will be a new man when this is over," I added, knowing in my heart what the real problem was.

As soon as I told Margaret she said she would go to Eastbourne with me to see Eric as soon as he was over his surgery. I knew that was what she would say and we decided to go and see Eric four days after his operation. Before I went I knew already that the operation had disclosed a very large cancerous growth, which had been the cause of the collapse of his kidney. This had now been removed, together with the kidney and the surgeons hoped all would be well. Like them I hoped so, too, but deep down inside me I knew he was living on borrowed time, though I put this thought at the back of my mind as best I could.

Margaret and I went to London to stay with my cousin Audrey at Morden, who went off to teach her pupils early next day as we prepared to leave for the train to Victoria. When we reached Victoria we had to use the escalators. I knew I could not walk Vida on to the escalator so while Margaret took our overnight bag I asked a passing traveller if he would be kind enough to put his hands at the back of me to provide balance while I got Vida on to the escalator. "I'll help in any way I can," he told me, so I bent down and scooped Vida, who then weighed seventy-three pounds, into my arms, and walked forward as the man steadied me as I got on to the escalator itself. I then put Vida down on it and when Margaret warned me I was nearing the top I picked Vida up again, the man steadied me once more, and I got off, putting Vida again on the floor, and thanking the stranger who had helped me.

We now caught the train to Eastbourne and went straight to the nursing home where Eric was. While I stayed with him Margaret took Vida for a run on the beach. Fortunately Vida did not like the sea at all and would always get at the back of anyone walking along the shore with her, as the breaking of the waves frightened her. So I had no fear that she would wade in and come to harm. When Margaret returned from her walk with Vida we went out for lunch. I then went back to see Eric while Vida had another run before we caught the return train for London. To get across London to Euston meant we had to use a descending escalator, which I thought would prove too difficult for me alone. So I looked for another man who I asked to steady me while I got on it with Vida. Scooping Vida into my arms again I stepped on to the escalator, nursing her all the way down this time, because I knew if I put her down in front of me I would never be able to pick her up again at the bottom. Even more pantingly this time I said "Thank you," to the stranger who helped me as he went on his way.

The first underground train which came in was packed so Margaret urged us to wait for the next. As this was not nearly so full we got on it. I kept Vida close to my legs but it became very full. "Come on, you'll have to come up on mum's knee," I told her, so I bent down, picked her up and Vida sat on my knees as though she did this every day of the week, whereas she had never been on my knee before. At Euston there was another long ascending escalator to negotiate and another, shorter but descending one, both of which I coped with. When I reached the top of the second one I was exhausted, partly I guess because I was so anxious about my brother. "There's a seat," Margaret pointed out, so we sat down and when she whipped out a flask I was glad to have the whisky she offered. I'd never needed a drink more in my life. What a journey!

My brother recovered from his operation, Iris, my sister-in-law, also recovered from her hip replacement operation and they began to recuperate together. At Easter 1983 Vida and I went to stay with them in Sussex over the holiday weekend. It was a delight to see Iris walking without a limp and my brother beginning to feel his former self. Now that their dog, Trudi, had gone they had a new one called Gemma, a puppy Eric had brought up, so she identified more with Eric than with Iris. Gemma and Vida were great pals and had a fine time together, so we all had a happy Easter in one another's company.

By May 1983, when Vida was twelve years old, I had another after-care visit. Though she still worked extremely well she was clearly becoming an old lady. When the trainer came to see us he told me he thought Vida's work was harder for her and it was asking too much of her to carry on. She would therefore have to be retired. Naturally I was very sad to hear his judgement, but I had come to realise over recent months her work was probably making her too anxious and causing her too much strain, too, even though we did not now go for the long walks which had been such a feature of our life together.

I agreed, therefore, that Vida should stop work and retire.

Chapter 8

Rosie and Tyler

Never before had this problem occurred. Lady had died after an operation. Shandy was put to sleep at the very old age of fifteen. Lippe had been sent back to the training centre and went out later to work in busy Manchester, while Mandy I had lost tragically. It appeared I had three alternatives when I agreed that Vida should retire. One was to keep her myself. The second was to let her go to a friend, or relative. Thirdly, the Guide Dog Association itself would find a good and suitable retirement home for her.

I did not have to think hard. I knew for certain I could not let

Vida go into a retirement home, for I would not be able to part with her on those terms. Could a friend have her I asked myself? Margaret would have taken her and Vida, I knew, would have been happy with her. But I did not think it fair, either to Margaret or to Vida and me, for us to be seeing each other many times a week and live almost cheek by jowl. So I decided to keep Vida and also have a new guide dog.

The Bolton Centre promised to look out for one for me. But they also told me I could use Vida for two very short journeys, one to my friend Doris, the other to Margaret. I had to cross only my own road to reach either of their houses, so it was agreed no strain was involved at all for Vida. From that day onwards I never asked Vida to do more than to go either to Doris or to Margaret with me. If I went further afield, when a friend could not pick me up, I went by taxi. Vida after all had done so much for me, and also given me so much over many years, I had to be scrupulously fair to her.

I was now without a working guide dog. It came home to me profoundly again how different life was when you had such a dog. Yet I still had Vida's company and we still loved one another and were happy together. Then in early September I was asked to go the Scottish training centre at Forfar because they thought they had a replacement suitable for me. I was rather disappointed because I had been so happy at Bolton and had such a high regard for the work there but as the Association said there was a suitable dog at Forfar for me I accepted their decision. Margaret said she would have Vida for three weeks while I was away being trained and Hilda travelled to Dundee with me where I was to be met by a staff member from Forfar.

I soon came to appreciate what a good centre it was. The

food itself was splendid, with home-made buns, or scones, for morning coffee breaks. After two days or so I was introduced to Rosie. She was a small Labrador, and mid-coloured, very wriggly and lively. She was also rather immature, being only eighteen months old and when she was on the floor lying on her back and flailing her legs in the air you would have thought she was only six months. I started work with Rosie, but did not find her very confident. I could see readily how different the situation was from when I had begun training with Vida. But then, I thought, Rosie is a different little girl. Inevitably it will take time, patience and perseverance. I must cultivate all three. Yet I wondered to myself how on earth I was going to keep Rosie quiet on the journey from Dundee to Crewe.

We passed our final test together and Hilda came to Dundee to travel back home with us. Once on the train Rosie curled up at my feet on the floor and never moved until we reached Crewe. I couldn't believe it: where was the bouncy, wriggly little girl I'd known? Once she left the training centre she seemed to have left her real self behind. We got into Hilda's car at Crewe and took Rosie to the woods near Hilda's home to give her a free run. I took off her collar and lead and put her free running collar round her neck, which is an ordinary dog collar, with a couple of bells on it so you can hear where your dog is.

"Come on, Rosie, have a good run," I said encouragingly. But she just plodded along quietly. "This dog has never been in the country before, Joyce," Hilda observed. "She's looking at the trees as though they are monsters." "Hilda, she has been in the country," I replied. "I've been out with her from the Forfar training centre. She's run and she's thoroughly enjoyed it." "Well," said Hilda, "she looks absolutely terrified in the woods here." "I just don't understand this," I thought as I put Rosie back in the car.

I had been advised that Rosie and Vida should meet on neutral ground first so Margaret had taken Vida over to Hilda's house, given her a run and was there waiting when we arrived. As Margaret saw our car arriving she had Vida stationed at the top of the drive. "Look, there's your mum coming, Vida," she observed. Vida looked up and saw Rosie with me and all her hair stood up on her back. I put Rosie on one side of me in the car and Vida on the other, Vida with her back to me, looking out of the window. But she had become a dog I could not recognise.

Eventually we arrived home and I brought Vida and Rosie in together. I fed Vida first out in her run, keeping Rosie in the house. Then I brought Vida in and took Rosie out for her food. As she was in a strange place I stood with her. She wouldn't eat. "Come on, Rosie, have your supper, there's a good girl," I coaxed. "No," she seemed to say, "I'm not having anything to eat."

Now I had been told at the Forfar centre she had to have Wilson's Dog Food, which is a dried product on which you pour hot water. And that under no circumstances was she to have tinned, or any other type of food. I tried again to get Rosie to eat her supper, but she would not have anything to do with it. I tried to understand the stress she had experienced - she had after all left the training centre, travelled all the way from Dundee, come to a strange new home and then to cap it all met a new dog. It was therefore hardly surprising she was responding in this way. The evening proceeded in this unhappy way. Vida was so miserable and Rosie remained ill at ease and definitely not at home.

There were two dog beds in my room by this time and I took them to bed separately and settled each down for the night. I cannot say I had much sleep myself as I tried to keep an eye on both of them. In the morning I took Vida down first, put her in her run with her breakfast, then had Rosie with me. I brought Vida in, took Rosie out and gave her breakfast. Even though I stood with her she would not touch it. "This is difficult," I thought to myself. I waited for her to do her toilet, then brought her into the back porch. "Come on, Rosie, you must have some breakfast," I said sympathetically. "Or you'll be a hungry girl." I picked up a handful of food, which she nibbled at; then another handful and she nibbled at this, too. I spent some twenty minutes feeding her, but she still only ate about a third of her breakfast.

Vida's hair had not gone down. It was still standing on end as it had done when I'd first met her with Rosie the previous day. I could still not recognise her as my dog. She was different and also miserable. To add insult to injury Rosie kept mounting her and instead of Vida turning round and saying "Grr! Get away you horrible little thing," she merely stood there and seemed to say "Mum, she's doing it again. What am I going to do?" Things continued far from easy but next day I went out with Rosie though she was far from confident, even though we only went on easy walks. I deliberately did not go too far, either. Instead we went out twice a day for short trips but still she would not eat a single mouthful. I therefore rang up the Forfar training centre and asked if I could try her with any other food than the type prescribed. "No," they told me firmly. She was allergic to food other than Wilson's and had to have that. I was urged to persevere, which I did, but although I had Rosie for six weeks, she never once ate a mouthful of food on her own accord, only food I fed her by hand.

Vida meanwhile stayed as unhappy as ever and I think in a doggy way told Rosie she was not wanted, had never been wanted, and should go away. Rosie was miserable, too, and to say I was miserable and worried was the understatement of the year. I therefore contacted the Bolton training centre, who did not know Rosie, and the staff there suggested things I might do to ease the situation, which I tried. But we were plainly getting nowhere.

With Vida, Rosie and me so unhappy, Rosie not working well and not eating properly either, things were most unsatisfactory. I don't suppose I was working with Rosie well either by now, because I was so worried and unhappy myself. To add to my unhappiness I now heard that my brother's cancer was affecting his knee and that he had to go to hospital for a knee operation. In no way could I go to Sussex to see him and take the two dogs with me. I worried about this for twenty-four hours. "Please, God," I prayed, "Show me the way forward. I just do not know anymore." I was getting ready in my bedroom, indeed was brushing my hair, when a voice came to me and said "A guide dog should be a great joy, a great help, too, and not a worry and an anxiety. Rosie must go."

It was as though a great weight had been lifted from my shoulders. I went to see Doris who asked how I was. "Doris, I've made a decision," I replied. "I've decided Rosie must go." "Thank God you've seen it," she said. "None of us could tell you that's what you must do. Now don't you dare alter your mind." "I won't," I promised. "I know now that is right." I now rang up the Guide Dog Training Centre at Bolton and spoke to the controller, explaining the situation. "Very well," he said, "We'll send someone over tomorrow to collect Rosie," which they did.

The Bolton centre did not know Rosie before she had come from Scotland but they had her for a few days in kennels. She wouldn't eat her Wilson's there either and so they put her on some other food which she did eat and which suited her. They took her out in harness and her work was not satisfactory. But they kept her and persevered with her though in the end she did not make the grade and became a very happy pet dog, where she was the only one and much loved.

On the day Rosie went back Vida was a new creature. She was happy again and there was light, happiness and laughter in the home, which had been absent for several weeks. But what was I to do? I could only go to two close friends who lived nearby. Yet I wanted to do many other things. "Joyce," I told myself, "You will have to do something you vowed you never ever would." I'd always said to myself and to my friends I would never use a long cane. "I won't have a white stick" I had told people many times but circumstances alter cases, so I told myself to sink my pride and have one. I made some enquiries but there was no-one locally who could give me the necessary training. But there was a person in Rhyl, some thirty miles away and arrangements were made for her to come and give me lessons. For five consecutive mornings one week, therefore, I went out with this long white cane. I found it so difficult but the lady helped me and told me on the fifth day it was up to me and what I needed most of all was practice.

Margaret came out with me. One day I was going down a road opposite where I lived and at the bottom of which is a right hand corner. I went on and on saying to Margaret eventually "Am I ever going to come to the corner and turn into Camberley Drive?" "You're in Camberley Drive now," Margaret told me. I had apparently come round the corner with my long cane and had no idea this was what I had done.

Margaret was normally working at the hospital where she was Principal of the North Wales School of Radiography. So I had to learn to get on by myself. I therefore began going out alone. Yet I found it so difficult and other people made it even more difficult for me, though they did not mean to. Everybody was used to seeing me out with a guide dog walking along confidently, being totally independent. Now here I was struggling with a long white cane. I would perhaps go up my own road, see nobody, turn on to the main road and then someone near me would say "Hello, Miss Dudley," or "Hello, Joyce, where are you going? Come along, take my arm." And I'd had to respond "Thank you very much, but if I don't persevere, I will not master this thing."

On and on I struggled, down past the shops. It was so difficult. But I managed to get home again eventually. I suppose about the fourth time I was going down the main road and round the shops when I turned onto the grass verge in the tree-lined avenue only to hear somebody say unthinkingly "You're not getting along very well today, are you?" "No, I'm afraid I'm not," I admitted. "It doesn't look like you," came the response. "It doesn't feel like me very much," I replied.

I was now on the verge of tears when suddenly I heard someone running along. A man who had been a patient of mine at the hospital, and subsequently a private patient, now came up to me. He put his arms round me and said "Come on, I'll take you home in the car. Ah, where's your dog?" "Dewi," I said, "don't be nice to me, please, you'll have me in tears." "Come on love," he persisted, "I'll take you home." "No," I told him, "I can't come in the car." "Why not?" he asked. "If I go in that car now I will never ever go out with this cane again," I explained firmly. "I've got to, so thank you very much Dewi, but please let me go on." I struggled forward and came home. But to myself I thought "I cannot go on like this."

"Now what you will have to do," I told myself, "is go out after dark. There will not be many people about and nobody will see you from a distance." I therefore began doing this, which was in one way advantageous. But in the residential roads immediately around me, with very little through traffic, there was not much to orientate me so I got lost once or twice. I did not know exactly where I was even though I could hear traffic in the distance. I therefore found I had to get closer to the sound and when I reached the road consider which one it might be. I knew bits of the trees in some of the gardens I passed so I would feel them with my hand and so reach home.

With this degree of perseverance I did improve and with my white cane was able to get to the local shops and also to go and see another couple of friends. Thus I regained a measure of independence; but when I consider what a white cane can do compared with a guide dog there is no comparison. I now therefore felt very blind and very inept, which was most unlike me. I had no confidence at all and found the situation was diminishing me as a person. For Vida's sake, of course, I persevered all the more. She was now getting shaky and lame in her back legs and becoming a rather old lady. "Unfortunately," I thought, "I will not be having her much longer."

Then in June 1985, after I had been down to see my brother again with Margaret and Vida, he died. I went to London to stay with my cousin Audrey and a friend who lived in London looked after Vida for the day, while my aunt, Audrey and Margaret and I, went to my brother's funeral. I then collected Vida on my way back. Next day, en route for Euston, Vida slipped on the escalator and was very frightened and disturbed. I gave her a veterinary tranquiliser but as Margaret and I were leaving the coffee lounge Vida gently fell to the floor and we found we were unable to get her to her feet.

Help was soon obtained and two porters carried Vida on a large board through the station concourse and then on to the train. She was flat out in the gangway all the way to Chester where we were being met by a friend. Margaret and I together, with the help of a willing passenger from the train, rolled Vida in my Danimac and carried her to the estate car. That afternoon I had the vet to see Vida but he was rather despondent about her chances of recovery. Margaret came to have a snack with me which consisted of cheese on toast. We had only just started when Vida wrinkled her nose and wakened . She had her own cheese on toast so I now felt more hopeful. I sat with her all night in the kitchen and when Margaret came round next morning she lifted her head and we helped Vida to her feet. She staggered out to her run and by the next day was her old self once more.

I felt my brother's loss keenly. What I would have done without Vida to comfort me and share my grief I do not know. Looking back now I feel she soldiered on to support me at that time. During the next eleven months we showered her with love and spoilt her which she loved. But by 1986 it became apparent Vida had to leave us. She had grown very lame and was becoming incontinent, too. Reluctantly I rang up Howard Davies, my vet, a man I greatly respected. "Howard," I told him, "the time has come when Vida has to go." He came to my house, I cuddled her as he gave her an injection and she went slowly down on her rug and passed peacefully away. What a wonderful, brilliant dog she had been! It was hard to part with such a lovely animal, but we had to say goodbye. Though it was very quiet and lonely without her, life had to go on and so it did.

While I'd had Lady I had been abroad and my mother had looked after her for me. When I had Shandy and Mandy and gone abroad on holidays Iris had cared for my dogs, either at her home after my mother died, or in our home, to which she had come to look after my mother. Having lost Mandy so tragically, when I had Vida I felt I was not able to leave her and holiday abroad, so in fact had not left Britain between 1972 and 1986. Now Margaret and I had a holiday in Switzerland that September while I was waiting for news of a new guide dog. Unfortunately I had to wait rather a long time. I was, of course, asked my preferences and had indicated I would like a Labrador bitch, hopefully a large one.

In January 1987 the North Western Regional Supervisor, Mike Johnson, rang and said he had a dog he thought suitable for me. "I'm sorry, Mr Johnson," I had replied, "I don't want a dog. I would prefer to have a bitch." "Well, you may have to wait some time longer," he indicated, which I said I was willing to do. "I won't have a dog, thank you very much," I told him. So that was that.

In June Margaret and I had another holiday abroad and when I arrived back the following day I received a phone call from Bob Steele, then training manager at the Bolton Centre. "I think I have a very suitable dog for you, Miss Dudley," he said. "What do you feel about it?" "What breed?" I asked. "A big Labrador, with a lovely temperament. I feel it would suit you very well," he repeated. "Did you say a dog, Mr Steele?" I asked. "Yes," he replied. "Mr Steele," I said firmly, "I don't want a dog but a bitch please." "I think he would be very suitable for you," he reiterated. "Mr Steele," I explained, "I'm not as young as I was. This may be my last guide dog and I was looking to having another bitch." "I just wish you see this chap," he persisted. "He's super. Don't make up your mind now. I'll give you a ring in a few days." And with that he put down the phone.

I was now in an absolute tiz waz, wanting a new dog badly, but a bitch. Partly my quandary was because I had known Bob Steele for a long time and had a great respect for him. I therefore grabbed my long cane, which I had christened Fred, and went round hot foot to Margaret to tell her of my dilemma. "Oh dear," she responded, "You have got a bit of a problem, haven't you?" "It's Thursday now," I commented "and Bob is going to ring me up on Monday morning for my answer. But he did say when he spoke to me he wished I could come and see the dog he had in mind." "We'll go and see him next week," Margaret said firmly. "See if you can make an appointment to meet both Bob and the dog next Wednesday."

I waited for him to ring on the Monday and told him I had given the matter much thought and as he had suggested I met the dog could I do this on Wednesday afternoon? "Be here at 2 o'clock," he said. Margaret and I therefore arrived at the Bolton Centre in good time and were shown into Bob Steele's office. After a few exchanges he told me he still thought the dog he had in mind was right for me. "Anyway, you must see him," he added. Accordingly he rang up the trainer and asked her to bring the dog in. Soon a very large, pale coloured Labrador appeared, walking in a very quiet and superior way. "Hello, what's your name?" I enquired. "His name is Tyler," I was told. I tickled his ears and told him he was a lovely boy. Then I said to Bob Steele I had a couple of biscuits in my pocket and asked if Tyler was allowed one? "Yes, he may have one," Bob replied. "Tyler, sit,"

I said. "There you are - there's a nice bikky." He liked it. "You think he's a nice lad?" Bob Steele asked. "He seems to be," I answered.

"It's no good looking at him," Bob went on, "You'd better come out and see how you get on together." Taking the dog lead in my left hand, and Bob's right arm, we walked through the entire centre. Tyler walked beautifully, head up and very quiet. He was put in the back of an estate car while I got into the front with Bob, who drove only a little way before we got out of the car. Then Bob put Tyler's harness on because I had only just met him. I had a check chain and lead with the harness and Bob put another check chain on with the lead. "Right, off you go across three side roads," he instructed. "Then you'll be up to the main road." We started off, got down the first kerb and Tyler sat. I listened for traffic, then told Tyler to go "Forward." He got up and moved over the road. At the next side road he sat again. I listened for traffic, then moved across, employing the same procedure in relation to the third side road.

Now we had to go up the main road. When we reached it Bob Steele bent down, took off Tyler's check chain and lead, and said "Right, off you go. A right turn here and along the main road, which you should keep on your left. Then go over three side roads and on the far side of the third get your dog to sit, do a right turn and find your way back to the training centre."

Fortunately I had known the way down Devonshire Road where we had to walk to reach Centre from previous visits. So off Tyler and I started. I had only met him ten minutes earlier and now I was crossing roads with him but we seemed to be responding well to each other. I said "Sit," which he did, then did a right turn, then trotted beautifully down the road in question. At another corner he sat, then we did the left turn, which put us on the right way for the centre. Tyler sat on the kerb outside the centre. I then said "Forward" and he got up and off he went. "Find the house, find the house," I urged and he walked down the drive, past a house on the right, then turned right and proceeded to the verandah outside the grooming room where there was a little step. "Find the step, find the step," I called out. He found it and sat down. I put his handle down and bent down to give him a big cuddle. "Oh Tyler," I told him, "You're lovely." Bob Steele asked me what I thought of Tyler. "Oh, Mr Steele," I replied, "He's absolutely gorgeous." "Right," Bob said to a colleague, "put a notice round his neck saying "Sold."" Turning to me he said "We'll have you back in a fortnight for him."

There followed two weeks of great excitement as I looked forward to having Tyler. I had no experience of working with a dog before but the moment I met Tyler I fell for him. When I had been training with him, one of the trainers of the class of eight of which I was a part had said to me "I watched you come in with Tyler the day you came to see how you got on and when I saw you together I thought you must have been working for a couple of years." In fact it had been twenty minutes.

Our training at the Bolton Centre had indeed been excellent. We did all the usual things, quiet roads, busy roads, right hand and left hand turns; also right angle corners, very sweeping corners and also lifts. We had gone to Woolworths, Marks and Spencer, the Market, as well as walking down busy streets and roads and crossing them, using zebra and pelican crossings. At the end of my three weeks we passed our final examination and I then brought Tyler home. Bob Steele himself came the following week three times to see how we were getting on.

Chapter 9

More of Tyler

Tyler was a little hesitant at first but I learned he had been out with someone else who could not cope with him and he had gone back in his shell. I think when he came to me he must have thought to himself "Oh dear, I wonder if I am going to stay here." But stay with me he did and soon we were working extremely well together.

Tyler was not as brilliant as Vida but turned out to be a very good and steady worker. He kept his mind on the job in hand, was never distracted by other dogs and always had his ear on what I wanted. He also turned out to be a delightful character. I used to say to Margaret "I don't think I've got a dog at all. I've got a little boy with a dog's coat on," because he developed so many different ways from the bitches I had known.

In my lounge, for example, I had a dog bed where my dog could sit when were sitting quietly together. When we had visitors, however, and we were talking, Tyler, feeling a bit out of it, would suddenly leave his bed, put two paws on front of the cushion on the left and give a big heave. Then up would come his bottom onto my knee and there he was, a great big boy, sitting there. When I responded with "Oh' Tyler, you are a baby," his tail would drop down between my knees. When I spoke to him, ignoring my visitors, who were amazed at the antics, it would wag.

After I had been with Tyler for nearly a year there was an

open day at Bolton where guide dogs and their owners, puppy-walkers and interested people, met for a day of enjoyment and entertainment. I arranged to meet Tyler's puppy walker there, who was a doctor's widow from the Wirral. We met in the grooming room and she spoke to him nicely, delighted to see Tyler again. But he was not especially interested to see Sheila now that he was my dog. "How do you find him?" she asked me. "Has he any special ways?" "He's got many little ways," I replied. "For example, he loves sitting on my knee." "Oh dear," she answered, "I'm afraid he sat on my knee from the time he was a puppy. I thought when he went to kennels he would forget about that. Obviously he hasn't." "I don't mind a bit," I told her, "though he is a bit of a heavyweight."

Tyler, of course, did the things that many other guide dogs had done - shopping, going to friends with me and to guide meetings, too. I also gave talks to various groups and he accompanied me to them. Life was good again and though I had said I never wanted a dog he stole my heart.

After Vida went I decided that when I had a new dog I would have further holidays abroad. So in June 1988 Margaret and I went to Switzerland again. I had heard about kennels seven miles from Wrexham and had visited them one day before Tyler had come to me in July 1987. I told them I would soon be having a new guide dog and asked if they would have him if I went abroad. They had then shown me round the kennels and I asked my two friends Doris and Margaret, who were with me at the time, to keep their eyes open and not miss anything on our tour, for all I could detect was that the kennels were very clean and adequate. Each dog had its own hut which was its bedroom home. They had, too, separate runs. In addition, there was a big enclosure where dogs had facilities for exercise during the day.

We had liked the kennels so when my 1988 holiday was approaching I made a booking and took Tyler to the kennels, though I had much trepidation about my action. I brought with me his bed and a couple of rugs, his brushing comb and a bone for him to chew. He went into his bed nicely as he settled and I gave him a big cuddle, telling him to be a good boy and assuring him that I would come back. But you cannot explain to a dog what the future now holds so it was with some anxiety that I rang up the same evening, though I wasn't leaving until the next day, to find out how Tyler was. "He's settled down beautifully," I was told.

After a pleasant holiday I collected Tyler and was told he had been the perfect gentleman and not a scrap of trouble. To say he was pleased to see me was the understatement of all time. Indeed I had to lean against the car hard in case he knocked me over because he was so excited. I always asked at kennels when I left a guide dog with them not to feed the animal before I collected it because I always took my dog to Acton Park for a good free run to start with. In this way I found it jettisoned any pent up feelings and got more exercise than in the kennels. Tyler, who was a very tall dog, ran like the wind once in the park.

In the spring of 1990 each Friday morning Tyler and I had begun to go to a day hospice centre called Nightingale House, which was part of the Maelor Hospital in Wrexham. I had already heard about its work and now attended a fund-raising function, met the sister in charge, the fund raiser and the person responsible for volunteers. I told them I wanted to help if I could, though I would be unable to make cups of tea or push patients around in wheelchairs. But I was not bad at talking to people and certainly a good listener. I was told I would be welcome to offer whatever services I could.

Tyler and I now set off for our first morning on duty. The Maelor Hospital was at the far end of the town from my house which was too far for me now to walk. I therefore called a taxi and in the reception hall put on Tyler's harness. Then I turned down the corridor with him, walking down it like a dream. We found Nightingale House itself easily and were made welcome by its staff and introduced to the patients. The experience took me right back to the days when my previous dogs had walked me through the War Memorial Hospital when I was a physiotherapist and in uniform. I had lunch there and Margaret, who finished early that day, picked us up at half-past one. When it came to going for lunch there was quite a battle between a number of patients who wanted to escort me to the dining-room. Tyler I had to leave in the lounge as the dining-room was small but I collected him immediately after and then stayed with the patients, whom I found delightful, for another hour.

Each Friday a young girl called Ann used to come and do hairdressing for the patients. One day she came to me in the dining-room and said "Joyce, Tyler's growling in the lounge." "Growling?" I replied. "That's not like Tyler. I must go and see what's happened." Suddenly it came back to me that the previous week there had been a very sick man present, who was unable to have lunch in the dining-room but who had eaten sandwiches in the lounge. Tyler had sat and looked at him and, though unable to speak, he had clearly encouraged Tyler to share his lunch with him. Normally I would have said "Please will you not feed my dog," but I had not been prepared to say this on that occasion.

The next week, when I was going into the dining-room for lunch, I didn't say anything but took the precaution of tying Tyler's lead round the leg of my chair. Again the man was sitting opposite Tyler with his sandwiches and evidently Tyler had decided he would like a bite of them. He had found, however, he was unable to reach the man as before. Now Tyler had a way of "talking," which wasn't barking, saying "H'mm, h'mmm, h'mmm." This is what he was doing, indicating he would like a share of the sandwiches but was fastened to his chain. It was this noise which Ann had heard and described to me as "growling." "Tyler wasn't growling," I explained to her. "He was merely having a friendly word."

In January 1989 my close friend Doris suddenly died. I was with her at 4.15 p.m. and by 5 o'clock she was dead. I was terribly shocked. I had met death before of course in my immediate family but they had been ill before death claimed them so I had been prepared. I was not, however, in any way prepared for Doris's death. She was a great loss to the Guide Dog Association, who also mourned her passing, for she had worked at functions for many years and her late husband had chaired the local branch in the 1960's and the early 1970's.

Doris's son and daughter asked me if I would speak a few words about Doris at the funeral because we had done so much together and I had known her so well. I took Tyler to the funeral with me and when it was time to go up the chancel steps and speak I put on Tyler's harness. He then took me most beautifully up a little part of the main aisle, round the coffin with great care, then up on to the chancel steps from which I spoke. He then brought me back down the steps and round the coffin again to my seat. People must have admired him very much indeed.

Doris's daughter, Rosemary, stayed with me for three weeks while she was turning out her mother's house and I was able to help her greatly. One day we had a terrible fright when Doris's next door neighbour and another friend and I were helping Rosemary and I was on a chair in the pantry. Tyler was around somewhere but the door into the garden was open. We were very busy and I suppose were not keeping our eyes open. Suddenly someone said "Where's Tyler?" "Isn't he here?" I asked. "We can't see him at all," was the reply.

I came down instantly from my chair, went into the garden and called and called and called. There was no Tyler. We then looked all over the house. Again there was no sign of Tyler. The side gate was closed so clearly he had not gone out by the front of the house. Instead we discovered he had gone into the garden and disappeared. We all now called and called again; but there was still no sign of him.

Unfortunately Tyler had not got on his free running collar where there was a badge saying "Guide Dogs for the Blind Association," and the name of the centre from which the guide dog came and its registered number. I therefore rang the police and told them what had happened. They promised to keep a look out for Tyler. By now Margaret had come home from the hospital so I rang her and she said she would get her car out and start searching. She went especially into the cul-de-sac at the back of Doris's garden and searched there. It was here she found him - in a garden in which he was trapped. Immediately she went to the owner and collected him. I was completely shattered but I suppose I was partly to blame because he obviously felt left out when we were all so busy and had not taken much notice of him. What he had done we later found out was to investigate Doris's garden, then squeeze through a fence into the next one, then reached another neighbour's garden and been eabable to find his way back.

unable to find his way back.

Margaret and I had always listened to Songs of Praise, seldom missing it because we enjoyed it so much. In late September 1991 there was an announcement at the end of one programme to say that a week Monday there was to be a special service of thanksgiving in Westminster Abbey to commemorate its thirty years. I immediately said "Wouldn't it be fine if we could go to it?" Margaret thought about my suggestion and said we could only go if we could be assured of getting a seat, which was entirely sensible. I therefore rang up the BBC the following day and spoke to the Director of Religious Broadcasting. I told him I would very much like to go to the commemoration with my guide dog and also be accompanied by a friend. Could they assure me of tickets? They rang back the next day and assured me we would be able to get into Westminster Abbey and that an invitation would arrive soon. Moreover, someone would meet us at the Abbey's door.

On Monday September 30th 1991, at mid-day, Margaret picked up Tyler and me by car and we set off for Euston via Crewe. Once there I popped Tyler's harness on and we proceeded to the super loo. The attendant on duty waived the charge and in we went. There was no-one there so I suggested to Margaret it would be a good place to give Tyler his food. Out therefore came his bowl and he had his supper and a drink of water before we caught a taxi to Westminster Abbey. We went round the side of the Abbey and found a bed of evergreen shrubs with some rough grass under them. Here I let Tyler off his harness for his toilet. Once returned, I put his harness on again and we made for the west door where sure enough there was someone from the BBC waiting to greet us. All three of us went in together and Tyler and I walked past the Unknown Soldier's grave and up the central aisle of the Abbey, through the screen to our seats near the choir. Margaret and I found, as we sat down and Tyler settled himself by my side, people came in a stream to talk to him, partly because he looked so handsome and well behaved.

It was an impressive service, with an address from the Rev Dr Colin Morris. Afterwards we proceeded to the cloisters for delicious refreshments where we found all sorts of famous BBC people gathered. The time soon came, however, for us to leave so we found Tyler's patch again, let him loose, then went out into the main road and hailed a taxi to take us to Euston, where we climbed on board our train for Crewe. Margaret and I were very tired as we drove back to Wrexham from Crewe and I am sure Tyler was, too, but in quite a mammoth journey for him he never put a foot wrong.

The second time Tyler went to London with me was when my favourite aunt had her one hundredth birthday. She was to have a party in a school room of the Methodist chapel she had attended regularly and where my cousin Audrey is still one of its leaders. Again we travelled by car to Crewe, then by train to Euston. Putting Tyler's harness on in the station concourse we found a taxi with the help of a porter and on arrival were given a late breakfast by a friend of my cousin. The party was from noon to three and was fantastic. Most of my aunt's friends and people of her own age had died but there were some ninety people at the party to celebrate her one hundred years.

The schoolroom itself had been decorated beautifully with one hundred white carnations with a backdrop of greenery. Tyler and I walked round meeting people we knew, including some of my relatives, but also people we had never met before.

With Tyler by my side I found we were a focus so many came to speak to us. When I went to chat with my aunt, who had remained standing to receive all the guests, I thought she must be eighty-five rather than one hundred. When the party was over she went home with Audrey by car, which was not far away, and Tyler, Margaret and I walked there. Margaret took Tyler to nearby Clapham Common for a run after which we had tea with my aunt before catching a taxi back to Euston and the journey home. Again Tyler never put a foot wrong and looked as if he travelled to London every day for one hundredth birthday parties.

Tyler was again with me when I attended excellent outdoor musical concerts in the grounds of local stately homes near Wrexham. People were encouraged to take their own picnic and enjoy the music in a beautiful setting. Once Tyler laid on his rug on the grass under a large umbrella during a heavy shower and all those around him were most intrigued. For some years I have also attended several environmental classes which I have found fascinating. They included a number of field trips which Tyler loved and I greatly enjoyed because the tutors always went out of their way to describe for me what the other students saw.

In 1993 I took Tyler to see my vet, Howard, for his six monthly checkup. Howard began by looking at his nose, ears and mouth and went right over him. Last of all he got out his ophthalmascope and looked into his eyes. He took rather a long time over his first eye and also rather a long time looking at his other one. "I'm sorry to tell you," he turned to me and said, "but Tyler's got retinal haemorrhage." "Never!" I exclaimed. "I'm afraid he has," Howard told me firmly. "He must be seen by the Guide Dog Association's ophthalmic surgeon."

Margaret and I brought Tyler home from the vet. I

immediately rang up the Bolton Centre and spoke to the kennels manager there. He told me Dr Barnett from Cambridgeshire would be at the centre in two weeks time. "A fortnight is a very long time," I told him, as Margaret called me from the kitchen to say "We'll go to Newmarket with him." I therefore told the kennels manager we would take Tyler to Newmarket the following week if we could have an appointment. In half an hour the manager rang back and told us he had made an appointment in Newmarket for the Monday, for which I was very thankful.

Tyler was now to be seen at the Animal Health Trust in Newmarket. Margaret and I did not know the area at all, nor did we know where we might stay, so I rang the Trust and spoke to Dr Barnett's secretary, who suggested we contact a good pub half a mile from the Trust's headquarters. I rang its landlord, who was quite prepared to have us and Tyler, too. However, just before we were ready to leave the following Sunday morning, the landlord rang to apologise and say he had overbooked and had no room for us. He told us not to worry and that he would sort out something. "We may be closed when you get here," he warned me, "but nevertheless come to my pub and something will be arranged." I did not dare tell Margaret this for she had a long drive ahead of her on a very hot day so told myself I would break the news to her on our arrival.

The journey was not easy because of the heat. We were bathed in perspiration the whole time. I was concerned for Tyler, in the back of the car, but I had lots of fluid and to entice him to drink put some milk in it. We stopped at a service station and renewed his water and in due course arrived safely in Newmarket. When we reached the pub Margaret said "The place is closed, the place is closed." "Don't worry," I replied. "They did tell me it might be closed when we arrived. Go up to the door and knock." Margaret got out of her car and knocked on the door. When she came back she told me "There's a notice on the door for us." "Oh is there," I replied casually. "Yes, there's the name of a guest house about a mile away with directions how to get there," she explained. We set off immediately, found the guest house and, when Margaret returned from having talked with the owner, told me they could accommodate us for the night. "But the husband and wife are giving up their room for us." "Are they really?" I replied. "They are indeed," Margaret said. "And they are quite happy to take Tyler. But I don't like to tell you..," she added. "Tell me what?" I said. "I'm afraid we're in a double bed!"

Margaret and I had never slept in a double bed before and it was far from anything we would choose to do. She is an only child and I was an only girl so we were both used to our own beds. But for Tyler we would have slept on the floor. The owners made us most welcome and shut up their own dog so Tyler could have a run round their garden. We then fed him and went to the pub for an evening meal as we were only having bed and breakfast at our hosts. While we were having a splendid meal there was a terrific thunder storm. Fortunately Tyler did not mind these and sat by the side of my chair while I ate my dinner as cool as a cucumber. When we left the pub, however, the car park and the roads were flooded, so we had more or less to paddle to reach our abode.

Next day we went to the Animal Health Trust to meet Dr Barnett, a charming man who was so good with Tyler. He examined his eyes carefully, then stood up and told us our vet had been quite right. Tyler had got retinal haemorrhage. "But," he went on, "I am very impressed that your vet diagnosed the condition because it's something vets seldom see. It could have been overlooked easily." I looked at Dr Barnett and gave him a smile. "But Dr Barnett," I explained, "my vet Howard is one of your former students so I would expect him to be good." Dr Barnett laughed. "You must leave Tyler with me for a time and we'll do some tests," he told me. "I want to take his blood pressure and some blood tests. Perhaps you could pick him up about four o'clock this afternoon."

Margaret and I therefore went off into Newmarket for some lunch, then a walk in the park. At four o'clock we went back to the Trust for Tyler. "I am absolutely puzzled," Dr Barnett reported. "I was certain he would have an increase in his blood pressure. But he hasn't. We tested it, did a blood test, took a sample of urine, which I thought surely would have upset Tyler. We then took his blood pressure again and it was perfectly normal." "The results of the blood tests will be through in a few days time," he continued, "and I will be in touch with you then. But at the moment there is no need for Tyler to cease working. It's not affecting his sight and it will be quite safe."

Margaret and I returned to the car with Tyler and had an easier journey home partly because it was not so hot, though we arrived back very late. Nothing was in fact revealed by the blood tests and his condition remained a mystery. Dr Barnett, however, suggested I saw Howard every four weeks which I did. Mercifully the haemorrhage started to resolve itself, so we were very hopeful that through an unknown cause it had been a temporary condition which we hoped would not recur. Unfortunately six weeks later, when we went to see Howard for Tyler's regular checkup, he found some further haemorrhaging. We contacted Dr Barnett and again journeyed to Newmarket for a further investigation. This, too, revealed nothing, and again the condition resolved itself. It seemed an absolute miracle.

In August 1995 a new hospice at Nightingale House, in the grounds of the old War Memorial Hospital, was opened. For some years Tyler had been a favourite at Nightingale House and all the patients knew and loved him. Margaret, who had retired at the end of 1992, and I had been on the fund-raising committee for several years and now rejoiced with others at the beautifully furnished building with its sixteen in-patient beds. The last Friday in August was the first week of the day centre and Tyler and I visited it. Everybody was delighted to see us and we spent a very happy morning with the patients. Their courage, fortitude and sympathy for others and the help they gave each other, had to be witnessed fully to appreciate its depth.

I left Tyler in the lounge as I went for lunch and when I came back one of the volunteers said to me "Joyce, I think there's something wrong with Tyler." "Why?" I asked. "He's not comfortable," came the reply. "He's not been able to lie comfortably. I think he's favouring his right leg." I had a look at him but could not find anything myself, but could tell Tyler was not as he ought to be so rang up my vet again and made an appointment. Howard examined Tyler and told me he had some problems with his shoulder. "Has he a bit of arthritis?" I asked. "I would think so," Howard judged. "He's certainly got a sore shoulder." Giving Tyler an injection, Howard asked me to come in two or three weeks time for him to look at Tyler again. This I did and Tyler was given a further examination. "We must have him X-rayed," Howard said. This was done and Howard brought the films through to discuss them with Margaret, because of her knowledge of radiography, and myself. They both agreed Tyler had arthritis in his shoulder.

Tyler was a bit unhappy walking for a few days so we did not walk very far. Then he seemed to recover well. He had been put on some tablets and I also cut down his work because he was now ten. I now had an after-care visit. We did not go on a long walk together but one of the senior trainers who accompanied us told me when we reached my home again Tyler's had been "a perfect performance," which he had not been able to fault. I was so proud of him.

I now found I had to cut Tyler's work down further because when we went to the shops, though he was fine on the way there, as we returned he began to struggle. Clearly the journey was too far so we must go for shorter trips. In the early days after Tyler's arthritis was first diagnosed he was seen by an orthopaedic surgeon from the Veterinary Hospital in Liverpool who offered to operate. He told me it would be a big operation after which Tyler might have a completely useless leg, or even no leg at all after an amputation. I was very shocked and talked to Howard subsequently, indicating I could not put Tyler through such an operation as he was no longer young. "Am I wrong?" I asked him. "No," he replied, "I think you're right. It is the quality of life that matters." I therefore decided against it and kept on with Tyler's tablets.

Tyler was happy doing some work and enjoyed being in the garden and the few free runs that were possible. By 1996, however, it was clear he was having more problems with his shoulder. "Would you like to take Tyler to Newmarket for the Animal Health Trust to look at him?" Howard asked. I said I would and made the Trust yet another visit. Here I saw an orthopaedic surgeon who explained to me what it might be possible to do to help Tyler. Again it sounded as though a big operation would be needed and the surgeon himself was not sure of its outcome. "Leave Tyler here overnight," he suggested "and come and see me again next morning." Before I left, however, there was one positive moment when Dr Barnett came to look at Tyler's eyes and told me there was very little sign of the old problem with the retina.

Margaret and I went back to our guest house and returned next morning as asked. When Tyler was brought in he seemed a very old and sad dog. "I'm afraid we have some very bad news for you," I was told. "We have X-rayed Tyler and he has cancer, with secondaries in his lungs." I was shocked. "Of course you wouldn't work him," the surgeon said, "but you could keep him for another two or three months on drugs." "I won't do that," I replied, remembering Tyler's distress in the bedroom one night when I took him downstairs and stayed with him until the morning and another occasion when, lying in the kitchen on his bed, he had another period of agitation.

"I have to do something about this," I had then said to myself. "I can't push pills down his throat, he's too distressed. I must have something sugar-coated." So I'd run upstairs, collected two Nurofen tablets, and urged Tyler to take them as sweeties, which he did. In a quarter of an hour he had quietened again but then he had become so quiet I was concerned I'd given him an overdose. Next day I'd taken him to see Howard, who had said the only thing that could have happened was that it had been too much for Tyler's heart, but when he had tested him he was all right. When, therefore, I was now told Tyler had secondaries I was clear that I could not keep him any longer. "I will take him home," I told the surgeon "and I will have him put to sleep."

The following morning, after a very sad journey back to Wrexham, I rang up Howard early and asked him to come and help me. "I'll come with a nurse at about 11 o'clock," he told me. When I had Vida put to sleep she was buried in Margaret's garden because she had a much larger garden than I had. Here two neighbours had helped Margaret and I lay her to rest and I had planted a sun-kissed conifer where she lay, with snowdrops covering the spot each spring. But I decided to have Tyler cremated.

I had a dreadful morning waiting for eleven o'clock to come but I knew I had to say farewell to Tyler. I loved him too much to let him suffer. The person who was going to do the suffering was me. Howard therefore came as planned, clipped Tyler's foreleg, popped in a little injection, with me cuddling Tyler, and, as with Vida, he curled up, lay down peacefully and that was the end of Tyler's life. I was absolutely heart-broken.

Two days later Howard rang me to say that Tyler's ashes were back. I went to collect them and found they were in a lovely little wooden polished box. On its top was a brass plate which said simply "Tyler." Margaret and I buried the casket at the bottom of my garden. It was May 1996. In the autumn I planted daffodils there so Tyler now has a bed of them each year on the spot where he lies.

Chapter 10

Grant

When I lost Tyler I contacted the Regional Training Manager, Mike Johnson, in Bolton to tell him my news and sent the death certificate as usual, for each dog belonged in the final resort to the Guide Dogs Association. "Well, what of the future?" he asked. "At the moment, Mike," I told him, "I can't make any decision. My heart is so sad and I cannot think into the future or of anyone to replace Tyler."

Tyler had died in the middle of May 1996. I was due to have a holiday in Switzerland so I did nothing until I returned from it. As I thought it became clear to me that I could not live without a guide dog. The house itself, as well as myself, was lonely without one, especially as I am single and eat so many meals on my own. More than that my independence had gone again, the more so as I had lost the habit of walking with a long white cane, which I had determined never again to use, I hated it so.

I knew, too, I would lose my quality of life once my independence vanished. Then my confidence would go and I would lose my very self. There was nothing for it but to start all over again with a new dog. I rang up Mike to tell him my decision who immediately said he would visit me and give me a re-assessment, partly because it had been years since I had started working with Tyler and it was now 1996. I was older, too, and having had Tyler since 1987 perhaps somewhat set in my ways.

Mike arrived and took me out on a modified harness where he pretended to be the new dog. When we came home and had a cup of coffee and a chat he told me he thought Tyler was going to be a very hard act to follow. "He most certainly is," I responded. "I wonder if you ought this time to have a dog which has been out before and perhaps lost its master or mistress," he suggested, "maybe a dog who has lost them through illness. Do you think a four-year old would do?" I considered his suggestion but thought not. My decision was partly influenced by the fact that the years such a dog would be with me would be curtailed but more especially I did not want one which had belonged to someone else. "If you can find me the right dog," I pleaded, "please I'll have a first-timer. "Leave it with me," Mike said, "and I'll see what we can do."

143

Weeks passed by as I wondered when I would hear some positive news and then, when an old friend from Anglesey was staying with me, the phone rang and it was one of the trainers from the Bolton Centre to ask if I would be available next day as he would like to bring some dogs over for me to meet. "I can be here tomorrow morning certainly," I answered. "We'll be there about 10.0 in the morning," he told me and rang off.

I was naturally excited; so was my friend Gwynna; so, too, was Margaret when she came round and heard the news. The following morning Paul arrived from Bolton with another trainer and one trainee, accompanied by two dogs. After coffee and a chat they said "Right, we'll go and fetch in one of the dogs." Soon they brought in a big Labrador, very pale in colour, who seemed very pleasant. "Right, we'll go out and have a walk with him," they told me.

We walked round the block and managed reasonably well but when we got back they told me they thought the dog had walked rather too quickly for me at my age. So they brought in their second dog called Grant. He was a first cross Golden Retriever Labrador, with a coat the colour of brandy snaps, which was longer than normal for a Labrador, though it was not as long as those of a golden retriever. He also had a bushier tail than a Labrador and seemed very bright. We went out, Grant was harnessed and I went round the block with him. With Grant I got on much better. When we got home the trainers told me they thought Grant was suitable for me. What did I feel? "Well," I answered, "we seemed to get on very well when we were out walking." "You must appreciate he still has seven weeks of training to go through," they replied, "so he's not yet fully trained. But if you feel you could be happy together then we will suggest to Mike Johnson that you have Grant."

The following day Mike rang me up to check I had been happy with Grant, which I confirmed. He then told me they had allocated Grant to me and that I would be going to the Bolton Centre in September for my training. Once again, therefore, I packed and went there, this time to meet Mr Grant. I arrived on a Saturday and had Grant on Sunday morning, though we did not do any work that day. Having got to know each other for that period we began work on the Monday morning. To start with we took simple walks together, then did more complicated road crossings, right and left corners, square and rounded corners, and zebra and pelican crossings. Then we went down roads where there were butcher and fish shops on the dog's side to make sure he was not distracted and wanted to go in to look for a chunk of meat. We also went into stores, up and down in lifts, all of which went happily with little difficulty.

I did find Grant quite a pickle, however, different from either Tyler or Vida. These two had been rather aristocratic and laid back. But Grant had been in the habit of jumping up which he ought not to have done and which should have been cured during his puppy-walking period. So I had some difficulty trying to prevent him doing this. He would also grab my forearm when he was trying to show affection. This was all very well, I suppose, but he did grab it rather tightly, so I had to dissuade him from this also.

At the end of three weeks home we both came to Wrexham. The first week the trainer and trainee came three times and in the second they came twice. Grant and I took a walk to the hospice, round a residential area and on the third occasion we went into Wrexham itself. It was afternoon and the town was very busy indeed but Grant did extremely well. Though he was on strange ground for him he stood safely at the kerbs, crossed only when it was safe, and with the trainer's help I got him safely into Marks and Spencer and through its food hall, too, when it was busy. A very old pub was being re-thatched and there were bollards outside it so Grant had to cope with these, as well as a pelican crossing. We had nearly re-traced our steps and were ready to get back into the car, which had brought us to the centre of town, when a voice said "Could you do that again?" I said "Yes" to the trainer's request, who had noticed I had been a bit fraught at the end of our trip. So Grant and I accordingly turned round and repeated the whole sequence.

I suppose after some three weeks, by which time Grant had learned the routine at home and knew how to use his run, I went with him to church one Sunday morning to an early service, accompanied by Margaret. Because it was a long walk to the church we went by car, though I walked there and back with Tyler in his early days and with my previous dogs. We took Grant into the church to be part of the congregation and he behaved very well. We came out and began to walk home as Margaret and I had arranged, she agreeing to pick us up en route.

We came through the town centre quite well, not as easily as when there were people about because there was nothing much to orientate me and the area was pedestrianised, so there were no up and down kerbs to watch out for. We found the pelican crossing and went over and began to walk through the Guildhall grounds where there were no pavements either, only carriage-ways and criss-crossing paths. It was a very windy morning, which no guide dog owner likes because it masks sounds. I had reached some bollards through which we had to cross a road on a zebra crossing. Grant went through the first of these satisfactorily then somehow or other veered in a direction which I knew was wrong.

I stopped him and tried to turn him back and allow him to find the way. He made it clear he was sorry but he did not know the way. "Come on, there's a good boy," I soothed him. "You find the way for mum." Again he indicated he could not and seemed to turn off the route. "It's no good wandering around the grounds," I told myself. "I shall only get more lost, particularly as it is early on Sunday and there is no-one about to ask the way." Moreover, there was no traffic on the main road itself which would have helped me to orientate myself, or if there was I was unable to hear it because of the high wind. I stood there for about a quarter of an hour when Margaret rescued me. She had waited and waited at the agreed spot but when we had not turned up knew something was wrong so had retraced her journey. Now I took Grant a little way further, with Margaret keeping her eye on us both as we went through the two sets of bollards again, then over the zebra crossing which enabled me to proceed and meet Margaret half way home as planned.

I had this sort of difficulty with Grant on several other occasions. Going into the town he was perfectly all right but coming home those bollards became a problem, partly because they were at an angle and not very easy to circumnavigate. When my trainer came to see me again I explained the problem which had cropped up. He went through the process with me and said "Now, when you get safely through and are nearly at the main road, stop Grant and give him a little yeasty drop. Do that each time so it will be clear in his mind that when he has gone through the bollard safely he will get a sweet." This device worked wonders and to this day I always give him his sweetie. Bollards are nothing to either of us now but they were quite a problem when we started working together.

Another difficulty, which I have never experienced with my other guide dogs, was that Grant would not always find the gate to our house. Now if I cross our road from the far side I knew more or less where the gate was because I came up a side road, turned right, went some twelve steps, then crossed the road opposite my gate. But when I approached the house in the opposite direction and came along the road on the same side, it was very difficult to judge when we had reached it. Sometimes Grant would find the gate nicely but sometimes he wouldn't. Grant happens to be a guide dog who once wrong seems to get upset. He will then switch off and not even try, even though I do not express my alarm or rebuke him. I wondered what I could do; then hit upon the same ruse as I had used before over the bollards. So I began to offer yeasty on the doorstep once we had arrived home perfectly. After several weeks of perseverance we got the routine mastered and now Grant never misses the gate, whether he approaches our home from across the road, or up or down the road on the same side.

All guide dogs are naturally different and what is a problem for one owner is not for another. It also takes time for a dog and its owner to bond together so the guide dog knows exactly what is wanted of it. You come to understand, too, what your dog is telling you. When, for example, it goes along a pavement and then slows down and makes the outside edge of the pavement, it is clear your dog considers there is an obstacle in the way. You therefore turn your dog back, approach again, and if it repeats the same manoeuvre you say "Good boy, listen for the traffic," then "Forward." Your dog will then come off the kerb, round the obstacle and proceed. But before you become completely bonded, one unit in fact, you are not quite sure of your dog and your dog is not quite sure of you. I suppose something of this process happened in the relationship between Grant and myself.

When I first had Grant he was eighteen months old but his behaviour off duty was more like that of an eight months old puppy. He was very fond of rolling on his back and putting all four paws in the air. When he had been with me only three or four weeks Grant went with Margaret and myself to Manchester where we were to attend a training course related to our local community health council on which we both sat. He walked nicely in his harness into the building where we met and sat very well through the lectures and workshops. But when he got bored he rolled on to his back with all four paws in the air, which the rest of the group felt was very endearing. Now, of course, he is more used to meetings and training sessions and is always very well behaved indeed. Everyone knows him and speaks to him when his harness if off saying "Hello, Grant." They make a great deal of fuss of him and when a meeting starts he lies down and you would not know he is there. When he is in harness, however, I do not encourage people to speak to him as it can become very distracting for him and put me in a predicament. I have in fact always been firm with each dog. No tit-bits have been allowed so at meals there has never been any worry. Each dog has however had treats - chocolate drops after grooming for example.

Grant settled down well, too, at the hospice and its residents loved him as they had loved Tyler earlier. He is still somewhat puppyish when he goes there rather than the superior gentleman which was Tyler. Sometimes I am forced to say to him "You are an urchin, young man, an urchin. If you were a little boy you'd have snails and strings and chewing gum in your trouser pockets, I'm sure you would."

In January 1997, only some three months after I had brought Grant home from the training centre, my aunt died, having the previous September reached her one hundred and fourth birthday. Until the last two years of her life she had still led an independent and full life, but the last few months had been sadder. Then, suddenly, she collapsed and a week later died in hospital. Naturally I was keen to attend my aunt's funeral as I had known her well and was very fond of her. I knew it would be a long day for Grant if he came with me but I felt he could cope. Margaret and I set off from Wrexham at half-past seven in the morning, leaving our car at Crewe as usual and getting the train to Euston from there. Grant's harness was put on when we reached London and we then hailed a taxi and went to the west side of Clapham Common, where my aunt's house was located. Here we met with other relatives.

I gave Grant the opportunity for a scamper in the garden because we did not dare take him to Clapham Common itself for a free run. Tyler I would have trusted there, only having to keep an eye on him and say if he went too far "Tyler" and he would have come back immediately. But if I had taken Grant to Clapham Common for a free run he would have been on the west side when I first released him and on the north side in two shakes.

Soon we were getting into the funeral car to attend the church where the service of burial was being held. When we got out of the car I popped Grant's harness on and he walked me through the church most beautifully. He behaved perfectly during the service and also in the funeral car as we proceeded to drive to the crematorium. It was the same in the funeral car when we came back to the church for refreshments when many people came to talk to Grant and to admire him. He still had a little more work to do as we went back to my aunt's house for tea before getting our taxi for Euston, the train to Crewe and Margaret's car to Wrexham itself. We reached home at quarter to ten. It had been a long day for Grant and he was still young and frisky; yet he had not put a foot wrong. I gave him such a big cuddle and told him how good he had been and how proud of him I was.

All my guide dogs, except Lady, have lived with me in my present house, which has a garden, and I have never had any problems with them not staying in it. But I soon discovered in the spring that when Grant was free in the garden after a while he scrambled under the chain link fence into my neighbour's garden. I would be in the kitchen getting the lunch and I'd hear my neighbour shout "Joyce, can you bring the lead please." I would then take the side gate by the garage and June, my neighbour, would be holding Grant there ready to put his collar and lead on and bring him home.

I decided I must ask a workman to put some clips at the bottom of the wire which seemed to work for a couple of weeks but then Grant discovered he could still push the wire up and scramble underneath it. One day he scrambled through and was nowhere to be seen. My neighbour's back doors were open, however, so he took himself through them and into her house. He then walked into the lounge where June was sitting watching television. It frightened her but Grant was not at all put out. In the end I bought some short sticks and Margaret threaded these through the fence and pushed them into the ground. That worked well for three weeks or so when Grant again discovered how to bypass them. So we purchased yet more sticks. One day Margaret was fixing them at the bottom of the garden where the fence was less strong, lying under a very prickly pyracantha bush on her stomach. She looked up and there again in June's garden was Master Grant, watching her in action. She remonstrated with him but it seemed to have no effect. He still escaped so much we began to call him "Houdini." Eventually I put a stop to these escapades by growing more plants by the fence, putting in further sticks and now Grant is unable to go astray any more.

I have not been able to go for long walks with Grant as I had with my other dogs. Shorter walks I find suit me better now; but I do go out with Grant each day and am still able to visit friends, go to the local shops and also into Wrexham town centre, though not as frequently as I used to. When I do go there Margaret takes me three quarters of the way. I do the main shopping, then I am picked up on the way back. Grant has a free run, a minimum of one every week, which he adores and I am thankful to say like Vida and Tyler he never goes into water so the lake in Acton Park is no enticement for him, which is a great relief to me.

All my guide dogs have had items with which to play - rubber rings, or bones, though Tyler only had boiled shafts of bones because if he had a rubber bone he set about it until he had taken it to pieces. Unfortunately he had then swallowed a couple of pieces at one time which had made him sick soon afterwards. But Grant had a big Father Christmas, a rubber ring and two boiled bones, as well as a twisted rope with a knot on either end. I bought it for him in the first place to try and keep him interested in staying in my own garden and playing with it there.

Grant now has a fine army of toys which includes Porky. Porky is a child's small soft toy, a rather handsome, benign pig. Margaret and I were once having a coffee evening to raise some funds to send musical instruments to a school we had visited when we were in Kenya in 1998. I had a bag of prizes in my hall and a bag of biscuits and as I went upstairs to prepare I thought "Don't leave the biscuits in the hall that's not fair." Picking them up and popping them in the lounge I went to get ready.

Coming down again I told Grant he was not going out that night but had to stay in. So he had gone on to his bed in the kitchen and I had given him a biscuit. "What's that under my feet," I thought as I trod on some object. I bent down and discovered it was a little pig I'd put in the prizes bag. Eventually Grant had spotted or smelt it and taken it out. Then he'd chewed the label off and started chewing the pig itself. Clearly it could no longer be a prize. "I don't know what we can do with him," Margaret said when she came next day. "Terrible boy," I said, "Here's your porky." How he loves it! He chews and chews it, though he has not yet destroyed it. He has most fun when he rolls over onto his back and holds Porky in his paws.

By 1999 Grant had had several holidays with Margaret and me in different parts of Britain. He has been to the Lake District and also to Devon. He has been to stay with friends and is always as good as gold when he is away. He is always good during our car journeys, too, and can even be left in the car he is so amenable. Indeed he loves the whole experience. He likes going to Anglesey especially because Margaret and I take him for walks along the cliffs.

Guide dogs should not be tempted by food when working but no human being is perfect and neither are guide dogs. One early morning I was walking most of the way to the supermarket with Grant and was then to be picked up by Margaret. As Grant and I were on our way he suddenly lurched forward with his head down. Quickly I nudged him saying "No, leave it" and on we went. Grant sat at the kerb as we arrived at a side road perfectly. There was no traffic so over we went. He repeated this at the next side road and only took me over when the traffic had passed.

Ten minutes later we met up with Margaret as arranged. As we approached her car Margaret said she had seen Grant in her mirror as she passed us and that he looked as if he was panting yet it wasn't a hot day. Then she had seen that Grant's mouth was not properly closed. On investigation we found he had scooped up a large bread roll which was too big to swallow. As he had no opportunity to eat it he had just carried it while working with me perfectly.

All my dogs have thoroughly enjoyed their free running, which is an essential part of a hard-working Guide Dog's life, but none as much as Grant. He came to be with me in mid-October 1996 and until Christmas had a free run in the local park, or a nearby Country Park, which he greatly liked. He was very fast but even these runs paled into insignificance when on a lovely, sunny, Boxing Day Margaret, Grant and I travelled some twenty miles to a real country destination.

As soon as we were safely away from the car park, I let Grant loose. The path ran along the bottom of a steep and well-wooded gorge, and he set off like an arrow shot from a bow. He raced up and down the steep sides, disappeared from sight, then rushed madly, but safely, down to me before going off again. I realised then that Grant was a real sporting dog, very fast and adventurous, with confidence to have me out of sight for a little while yet always returning panting to my side.

Margaret and I sat on a fallen tree trunk and ate our turkey sandwiches while Grant lay flat out at our feet, panting. He walked again after lunch and when we returned to the car it was with a very tired but happy dog. The following summer we went to the Guide Dog Hotel at Teignmouth in south Devon. The first day there we went to the Dart Country Park, where again Grant enjoycd himself immensely.

In late afternoon he had streaked ahead as we were going up a slight hill, disappeared from sight, then turned back and came racing towards me, arriving at speed as he jumped up and put both his front paws on my chest. I was wearing a haversack and was on rising ground so over I went and fell flat on my back, or rather on to my back with the haversack digging very uncomfortably into my ribs.

Another day on that same holiday we went to Bovey Tracey, where Grant behaved rather like a mountain goat, leaping from rock to rock at great speed but with absolute safety. Never before had I owned such as athlete as a Guide Dog. One day we walked along the cliffs from our hotel and returned through a dell where there was a rather sluggish stream. Grant was running alongside when suddenly he went through thick black mud. He returned to us with the mud stuck to most of his body.

As we returned to the hotel, Grant now on a lead, we met the kennel girl who was on duty. We all laughed when she enquired how his lordship had got himself into such a state. "Give him to me," she said, and took him off for a bath. He returned looking splendid. I must confess that though we have been back there for further holidays, the dell has been strictly out of bounds.

When Guide Dogs are free running it is difficult to realise that they are the same dogs, who when in harness, are so steady and responsible. As a member of the North East Wales Community Health Council I attend a great number of meetings and Grant is always so well behaved. Everyone knows, loves and admires him. Recently at such a meeting, on arrival the Chairman spoke to Grant and said that at a meeting the previous week the Director of Special Health Services, Wales, had been asking after Grant. He had obviously made more impression on her during two days of conference than any of the human members present. Recently Grant attended a meeting of the North Wales Health Authority with me and as I collected my badge for the day, there was also one for Grant to pin to his collar. What a joy he is, not only to me but to all who meet him as he looks after me and shares my life.

Grant will be seven in March 2002 so if all is well I should be able to work with him until he is ten. I will not myself be very young in seven years time so what the future holds for us together I have no way of knowing. But I do know if the time comes for me to leave this world and Grant is still fit and well then Margaret will have him as a pet. He would miss me of course because he is so very attached to me. But he is also fond of Margaret, used to her home and garden and would settle down well with her.

As my journey reveals I have had many ups and downs during the years I have been a guide dog owner. I have had my share of worries and anxieties. There has been sadness, too, when I have lost my beautiful dogs but nothing in the world could have been as precious to me as them. They have given me freedom and independence, dignity and a quality of life which has enabled me to take my place in the sighted world on equal terms with men and women.

Epilogue

Guide Dogs - A Short History

The guide dog movement in Britain began, as many other pioneering ventures, in a rather makeshift way in 1931. Now it has four national dog training centres and thirty one local district teams. The small number of supporters at its start has become a network of over 450 fund-raising branches as well as individuals and other groups who help raise the money necessary to breed, rear and train the many dogs now serving almost five thousand blind people.

The movement began internationally shortly after the First World War. In Germany a few dogs were trained to help people blinded during the conflict, work which came to the notice of a rich American Mrs Dorothy Harrison Eustis, who was to use her money to help the growth of the movement substantially.

At kennels she ran in Switzerland she bred and trained German shepherd dogs for work with the customs service, the army and Swiss and Italian police. After a visit to Germany to see the guide dog training centre there she wrote an article about her experience for the American *Saturday Evening Post* in October 1927.

A blind American, Morris Frank, wrote to her as a result of this, saying he would like to forward the work in America so Mrs Eustis trained a dog for him at her kennels, arranged for him to come to Switzerland to learn how to work with the dog and sent him back to the USA.

In 1928 she set up a guide dog centre, L'Oeil Qui Voit, (The Seeing Eye) at Vevey in Switzerland and also established the first centre for training guide dogs in America. Travelling and lecturing widely about her work she began to develop awareness and support and by 1930 articles began to appear in British papers. Muriel Crooke, who lived and trained dogs near Liverpool, and Rosamund Bond, who had bred and exhibited German shepherd dogs, became interested. They met Mrs Eustis in London on 23 September 1930 when she offered to lend a trainer to run a trial scheme in Britain.

Land and a lock-up garage in Wallasey in Cheshire were rented and the first trainer, Mr G. William Debentez, arrived on 1 July 1931. By October the first British class had completed its training. Two more courses followed and in October 1933 training became more permanent when Captain Nicolai Liakhoff, once an officer in the Russian Imperial Guard, who had been working with Mrs Eustis, arrived. His service to the Guide Dogs for the Blind Association, founded in 1934, included roles as trainer, Director of Training and finally consultant until his death in 1962.

The early years were difficult, not only because of money problems. Dogs were not then working with the police, army or the RAF and many were in principle against making a dog work. Some of the first trainers were indeed abused and told what they were doing was cruel and useless. Gradually, however, as people saw how guide dogs changed the lives of the first trainees, the public ceased to be so hostile.

In the early days after much training had been undertaken many dogs were considered unsuitable but in 1956 a change occurred when the first puppies were placed with volunteer "walkers", who both looked after them and accustomed them to traffic and crowds, restaurants, transport and shopping. They were returned to their centre as young adult dogs for their full course of training. In the 1960's, besides the "puppy-walking," as it is called, a breeding programme was set up which now has its own centre near Leamington Spa. This was greatly assisted by asking volunteers to take the brood bitches, who now number over 260. As a result some 80% go on to become fully trained guide dogs.

To start with German shepherd dogs were almost always used, donated or bought. Now it is mainly Labradors who form the majority of the dogs in service, or labradors crossed with golden retrievers. Sometimes some German shepherd dogs are also used as well as pure golden retrievers or border collies. Their names are often chosen because they are clear and distinct when called out and given commands or requests.

The Association makes only a nominal charge for a dog so no one is excluded from owning one and offers, too, a feeding allowance as well as paying vet's bills. Ownership of the harness actually remains with the Association. It never loses touch either with the owners or the dogs, for whom aftercare is regularly provided, a colossal task in itself as there are almost 5,000 guide dogs in harness, with some 730 retired and nearly 700 in training. There are also some 900 puppies from a breeding stock of 260.

Money for all this work comes from diverse sources but the Association remains independent of the state. Costs include the increasing demand for guide dogs themselves, replacements for dogs who retire, or die, long cane training and advice on daily living problems. The Guide Dogs for the Blind Association can be found at

Hillfields
Burghfield Common
Reading
RG7 3YG

(0118 983 5555).